This book is to
the last da

MAY 04 G T	DE‌‌‌‌	F N FEB 18
SEP 04 C S	MAR 10 A S	C S FEB 19
JAN 05 C R	C Z SEP 12	A Z OCT 19
	3 0 SEP 2013	
JUL 05 B R	2 8 FEB 2014	
JAN 06 D P	B T FEB 14	
APR 07 B R	1 3 AUG 2014	
JUL 07 K S	A Z AUG 14	
NOV 07 D O	G T MAR 15	
MAR 08 A W	A W JUL 15	
APR 09 K N	F P DEC 15	
AUG 09 M R	B R JUL 16	
	2 4 MAY 2017	
	M X JUN 17	

ANGUSalive
Withdrawn from stock

Angus Council
CULTURAL SERVICES

FEB 04   U

STEP INTO MURDER

When beautiful fashion model Sonia Dixon disappears, photographer Brian Rawson becomes involved in large-scale theft and terrorism. His new contract with Wesloe's, well-known dress manufacturers, was to be a turning-point in his career; instead, it was a step into murder, for which he was the main suspect. To save Sonia and his career, Rawson must turn detective — but his only clues are a shoe lying in a pool of blood, a frightened girl who comes to him for help, and the murdered man's missing assistant.

SPENCER CURTIS

STEP INTO MURDER

Complete and Unabridged

LINFORD
Leicester

First published in Great Britain in 1971 by
Robert Hale Limited
London

First Linford Edition
published 2004
by arrangement with
Robert Hale Limited
London

British Library CIP Data

Curtis, Spencer
    Step into murder.—Large print ed.—
Linford mystery library
    1. Photographers—Fiction
    2. Detective and mystery stories
    3. Large type books
    I. Title
    823.9′14 [F]

ISBN 1–84395–205–X

Published by
F. A. Thorpe (Publishing)
Anstey, Leicestershire

Set by Words & Graphics Ltd.
Anstey, Leicestershire
Printed and bound in Great Britain by
T. J. International Ltd., Padstow, Cornwall

This book is printed on acid-free paper

Prologue

It was misty.

The mist wreathed about the road, and about the gently sloping fields which led down to it. It found its way in between the trees which formed a small copse near the road, just by a nasty bend; in fact, the trees were one of the reasons why the bend was nasty, and many schemes for their removal had been put forward. Now, in the mist, all traffic would have to slow almost to a halt.

One of the four men who were hiding in the copse chuckled. It was not a pleasant sound, and the man next to him turned.

'Do you have to keep making that noise?' he demanded.

The man chuckled again. 'You'd make it if you were thinking what I'm thinking.'

'What the hell are you thinking?' another man asked.

'I'm thinking about what the birds will

do for four blokes who've got ten thousand quid locked away. That's what we'll have when this job is done. Maybe more.'

'They won't do anything for you if you keep it locked away,' the third man said sharply. 'And if you think too much about them you won't have any money because you'll botch the job.' He fell silent, and peered into the mist as there came the sound of an engine. The vehicle came into view; a small saloon car, driven by a woman who gazed anxiously through the windscreen, and leaned forward to rub it as she came to the corner.

'If this mist thickens much more,' the man who had chuckled said, 'we aren't going to be able to see anything. It's all right now, but what's going to happen when it gets properly dark?'

'Quit worrying. We'll be through long before then.'

They fell silent. Two more cars and a horse box passed. The darkness grew, and the mist thickened slightly, visibility becoming worse.

Suddenly, there came the unmistakable

sound of a lorry.

The four men stiffened. One drew a nylon stocking from his pocket, and eased it gently over his head. After a moment, the others did the same, then they began to move towards the road. The lorry drew nearer. The engine roared as the driver changed gear for the corner, and there came a faint squeal of brakes.

Two of the men moved on to the road. One of them held a torch, which he flashed towards the driver's cab. The lorry seemed to slow, then speed up abruptly. One of the men cursed. He leapt for the cab, missed, and sprawled heavily in the roadway. The rear wheel of the truck brushed his outstretched arm as it went past, and he tried to squirm out of the way.

Suddenly, there was a crash, followed immediately by a cry and a sharper squeal of brakes. The lorry driver, striving to protect his cargo, tried to increase speed, peering into the mist through his broken windscreen, which had been shattered when one of the men had thrown a brick through it. The corner loomed up.

Conscious of the men clinging on to his cab, the driver swung the wheel. It was a good try, but he misjudged it slightly and felt the lorry running on to the soft earth at the side of the road. He slammed on the brakes, swung on the wheel, and the lorry lurched.

For a moment, it seemed as though it would turn over.

That was when one of the men opened the cab door, and struck the driver on the head with an iron bar. He slumped forward over the steering wheel. The last sound he heard before unconsciousness fell was a chuckle, which seemed to him incredibly sinister and evil.

1

Photographs

The room was completely dark. The girl stood at one end, on a specially made, low platform, waiting, smiling faintly, one hand on her hip.

A light flashed suddenly, blindingly, exploding into every corner of the high-ceilinged room, lighting up the girl briefly before it faded away. The darkness returned, but now most of the tension which had built up over the last few moments had died away.

The girl didn't move.

The main lights of the room came on.

Now, she moved, and it was as if she were completely exhausted, drained of all emotion. She walked slowly to the steps at one side of the platform and came down them, stopping when she reached the bottom. She took a deep breath, then moved forward quickly, towards the photographer.

'That's the lot for today, Sonia,' he said, starting to unscrew the lens from the camera body while Bill, his young assistant, jumped lightly on to the platform and began to sweep it with an old, almost hairless brush.

Sonia asked: 'Are there many more, Brian?'

'Lots,' answered Brian Rawson. 'These are only a first run to help them make up their minds what they want to do with the finished thing.' He looked faintly surprised as he added: 'You've been doing this for long enough now to know how many there are likely to be.'

'Perhaps I have.' Sonia Dixon smiled and ran one hand over the material of the dress she was wearing, a short, pale green creation which shone, as if it were made of some plastic material. 'I like to ask,' she said defensively.

'You can ask if you want.'

'Talking of asking,' Sonia went on, coming closer, 'have you got a new camera specially for the occasion?'

Rawson flushed. 'What if I have?'

She grinned. 'A new Minolta?'

He saw what she was getting at. Three weeks earlier, a lorry with a whole consignment of Minolta cameras had been hi-jacked. So far, all the cameras were still missing, though the police, realising that cameras as expensive as that could only be disposed of through trade channels, had sent a circular round to all photographers, asking them to look out for them.

Rawson said: 'I've got them all stored in the back room. I'm going to be like the oil millionaires are with cars.'

She frowned.

'They only use a car until the petrol runs out,' Rawson explained. 'I'm going to use each camera until the film gives out, then I'll get another one. It's better that way.'

She pressed her lips together, mock anger showing in her eyes. He dodged the blow she aimed at him, then he said:

'Much more of that, young lady, and I'll find a new model.'

Sonia's smile broadened; all trace of

7

the fatigue she had shown earlier seemed to have gone.

On the platform, Bill's brush banged against the wall.

'Seriously,' Sonia said, 'you suggested to Wesloe's that I should do these photos, didn't you?'

'Yes,' he answered cautiously.

'It's a big chance you're giving me, isn't it?'

'If you want to put it that way, yes. You'll be doing the new Wesloe Collection. The girl who does that usually does a lot of touring for them later, appearing in Paris, Rome, you know the places better than I do. You should do all right out of it.'

'You know I will!' Sonia exclaimed warmly. 'You want me to do well out of it. You must do, or you wouldn't have suggested it.' She reached up quickly, pulled his mouth down hard on hers, then slipped easily out of his grasp. Before he could recover she had left the studio and gone through the door which led to the dressing-room. She called to him, her voice muffled by the half-closed door.

'I'm glad it's you doing these pictures and not that Philip Roxy.'

Roxy was one of the other photographers who had been in the running for the contract on which they were working.

'Why?' Rawson shouted. He packed the lens into its protective case and slid it into the cupboard. As he leaned over the bench, a thick lock of hair fell into his eyes. He shook it back impatiently.

He was seven years older than Sonia, who was nineteen, although the open-necked shirt and brown trousers which he wore in the studio made him look younger than he actually was.

'I thought Roxy was a friend of yours?' he went on when Sonia didn't answer.

'He may have been once,' she replied, 'but he isn't now, not after what he tried to do the last time I was there.'

The dress had been too full at the waist and had had to be pinned at the back. She took the pins out slowly, letting each one drop with a faint ping into a glass tray. She ran her hands lightly over the dress to make sure they were all out, then tugged down the zipper and stepped out

9

of the dress. Standing on her toes in front of the long mirror, she twisted this way and that, unable to resist the temptation to show off the figure that had made her, in a little under twelve months, one of the most sought-after models in London.

She was shorter than the average model, and she had long straight, black hair, that looked as if it fell the way it did of its own accord, but which was actually more trouble to keep in place than the most complicated of styles. She moved one leg, her hands on her hips, and half turned.

She had been standing like that at Roxy's when he had sidled into the dressing-room . . .

Even now, she seemed to feel the touch of his pawing hands, and hear the crack of her hand across his face.

She picked up the dress and dropped it neatly over the back of the room's only chair. Nine months ago she had been more or less unknown, a model, but no different from the hundreds of other girls who paraded hopefully before the cameras. She had started by modelling dresses in the store where she had worked as a counter hand, and shortly afterwards she had done a successful test for an Agency. After working with them for a while, she had decided it might be more profitable to turn freelance. She had been right, and had become more and more successful.

The Wesloe Collection was one of the top modelling jobs.

When she had heard that Brian Rawson had got the contract, and that he had chosen her to work with him, she had been as excited as she had been when the store had first asked her to model for them.

Quickly, she pulled on her own pale blue dress, changed her shoes from the plain ones she had been wearing to her own, black, with a gold letter 'S' tooled on the toe, and sat down to mess with her hair for a moment. Satisfied that it was right, she took her top coat from the peg and went back into the studio.

The flash startled her.

Rawson grinned, working the transport lever on another camera.

'Just trying this new soft-focus attachment,' he said. 'A really good model should never be taken unawares.'

She said: 'And a really good photographer should always catch his subjects at their best.'

'You look lovely,' he assured her, 'but I'll tell you what I'll do.'

'What?' she asked cautiously, suspecting some trap.

On the platform, Bill grinned and tried to look as though he wasn't listening.

'I'll let you have the negative, on condition that you have dinner with me tomorrow night.'

She hesitated for only a moment, then nodded.

'We'll fix it up at tomorrow's session,' she told him. 'I'll have to dash off now. Half past ten in the morning be all right?'

'Half past ten will be fine,' he answered.

She turned, and Rawson watched her out. After the door closed he heard her heels clicking along the passage, and he pictured her going past the door to his own flat, past the work room, and into the reception room, then down the stairs to the street.

Perhaps they could go out to dinner tomorrow night. Perhaps afterwards they could come back to the flat for a while. Perhaps they could —

He turned as Bill jumped down from the platform.

'Shall I sweep the rest of the floor, Mr. Rawson?' he asked.

★　★　★

Outside, Sonia looked at her watch, even though she knew the time. The gesture was habitual now, and came from constantly rushing from one appointment to the next. Perhaps when she had finished these things for Wesloe's she would be able to work less for the same income. She thought this with the cynical, jaded air which came from having worked every day for three weeks.

The picture that Rawson had given her of the contract made it sound almost too good to be true. For a year, her face would be featured on all the publicity for

13

the Miss Wesloe dresses, as a kind of house image to help the public identify them. Wesloe's weren't a small firm, either; they controlled, directly or indirectly, about half the market.

It would be almost as good as making a film.

A taxi came slowly. She made sure that it was empty, then hailed it. The driver stopped easily in spite of the double line of traffic that he was in, and reached across to open the door.

She took a last look at Rawson's illuminated sign half-way along the street, smiled at the cab driver, and climbed in.

2

Missing?

By a little after ten the following morning the first clients had just left and Janet, the receptionist, had brought in the morning coffee. She left Bill and Rawson to drink theirs in the studio, and went back to see to one or two things in her own office. Rawson watched her go out, took a sip of coffee and put the cup down harder than he had intended. Coffee slopped over the rim, on to the table; he shook his arm as some of it went on his sleeve.

Bill watched.

Suddenly he said: 'Janet was at me again this morning, Mr. Rawson.'

Rawson looked round for something to wipe up the spilled coffee. If he left it, it would be certain to ruin some films before the morning was out. He found an old cloth and rubbed hard, his mind busy with the problem of Janet.

15

The trouble with any receptionist in a business like this was that she might fancy herself as a model. Janet had been 'at' Bill for nearly a fortnight now, trying to persuade him to talk Rawson into doing some pin-up pictures of her. There was nothing wrong with the idea itself — if she had been anyone but the receptionist. He never liked to get involved too closely with them; they were too near the clients, and if anything he did upset Janet, she could have a shattering effect on the business with a few off-hand words in the right places.

Of course, if he didn't do what she wanted now she would be upset, but she would still be careful, afraid of a definite refusal if she did anything wrong. That would have to be the technique; keep her on the hook until the idea burnt itself out.

Bill was asking what he should tell her.

'Leave it to me,' Rawson said. 'If you don't say anything she'll come to me herself and I'll sort it out then. Quiet,' he added as there came a sound of footsteps from the passage.

Janet came in.

'Finished with the cups yet?' she asked. 'I'll go and wash them if you have.'

'Sure.' Rawson passed over his empty cup and reached across for Bill's. Was it imagination or was her dress shorter than those she normally wore? He shook his head faintly.

She raised her eyebrows. 'Something the matter?'

'No.' He grinned. 'Nothing at all.'

She turned and left the room.

Rawson looked round. The next session was the one with Sonia and the last before lunch. The last for the day, too, as he had wanted to be certain of not being rushed with these pictures.

'We'd better have the platform ready,' he said to Bill. 'There's still a lot of junk on it.'

Bill moved across, took the hairless brush and began to bang on the floor with it. Rawson looked at his watch, then went to set up the camera.

It was half past ten.

He didn't start to worry until it was eleven o'clock, and Sonia had still not arrived. He had never known her to be late before, not even by a few minutes; she was too anxious to reach the top to risk a reputation for unreliability. Of course, she could be ill, but she had shown no signs of anything the day before, and in any event she could easily have telephoned. With a feeling of unease he told Bill that he was just going to see Janet, then hurried along the passage into the reception room.

Janet's desk was in one corner, diagonally across from the door that led to the stairs and the street. A deep pile carpet of quiet charcoal colour was on the floor, while two strips of moulding fixed along one wall held some of his best pictures. Two armchairs and some smaller ones, all black, stood around the walls, and a table with magazines on it, and a couple of filing cabinets in the corner, completed the furnishings.

Janet wasn't there.

He looked round the room, puzzled, then reached out for the phone on her desk and dialled the number of Sonia's flat. He heard the phone ring at the other end, then twisted round as the door from the stairs opened.

Janet came in, carrying the tray of cups, which she put down on the desk. Rawson replaced the phone, not surprised that there had been no answer.

'Where've you been?' he asked, irritable now.

She looked at him in surprise as she started to put the cups away in the bottom drawer of one of the filing cabinets.

'You know where I've been. I came in and said that I was going to wash the cups. There was only Sonia due, and she knows the way. Remember? Or are you getting forgetful in your old age?' She grinned mischievously. 'You're too occupied with thinking about Sonia to remember much, aren't you?'

He turned, almost savagely. 'What do you know about Sonia? Do you know where she is?'

Again Janet looked surprised. 'I'm sorry,' she said. She banged the drawer shut and sat down, making no attempt to alter the hem of her dress, which had fallen carelessly. 'I didn't — '

'I'm sorry too, Jan.' He saw the dress and glanced away. Normally, the joking wouldn't have mattered, would have been accepted and parried. Now, it seemed out of place.

She said: 'Where is Sonia, anyway?'

'She hasn't arrived.'

'Have you tried her place?'

'That's what I was doing when you came in. There was no answer.' Idly, he watched Janet cross her legs and smooth down the dress at last. He was certain she was throwing herself at him in an attempt to get him to take those pictures. The dress was a deep red colour, almost as short as the one which Sonia had worn the day before, and it went well with Janet's dark hair and complexion.

'I don't understand it,' she said. 'She was looking forward to doing those photos, she told me so yesterday. You don't think she's ill, do you?'

'She wasn't ill yesterday. Look, Jan, I've got one or two things to do in the workroom. Will you try her flat again in a couple of minutes and let me know as

20

soon as you get something?'

He went into the workroom.

Where *was* Sonia?

At twelve-fifteen, she was still missing.

3

Strange Visitors

At one o' clock, Rawson had a quick lunch in his flat, then returned to the reception room, where Janet was sitting at her desk, eating sandwiches and drinking tea from a flask.

'Anything from Sonia?'

'Nothing yet.' She finished a sandwich, then seemed to hesitate before adding: 'You're really worried about her, aren't you, Brian?'

'I am.' He perched on a corner of the desk, a favourite place to sit when he was discussing things with her. 'We were supposed to be going out tonight to celebrate the contract.' It sounded better that way, more like a business dinner. He hesitated slightly, then went on: 'Look, Jan, I've got to see Yates sometime about those negs he wants. I may as well go this afternoon, and drop by Sonia's while I'm out.'

He left shortly afterwards, but after spending nearly an hour with the talkative Yates it was almost half past three when he finally arrived at Sonia's flat. He parked his nearly new Triumph sports car, got out, and took a quick look at the house numbers. It took him only a few minutes to find the flat, one of three built over a block of new shops in Chelsea. The entrance was at one end of the row; as he approached it, two women with prams stopped to talk, blocking it. One of them saw him, and turned her pram so that he could pass. He half turned to pass through the gap, and went up the stairs.

They led into a pale pink corridor, which smelled strongly of new paint. Sonia's door was painted white, with a large, black figure '2' in one corner of it, and a black bellpush in the centre. He pressed this, then waited a few moments before pressing it again. He heard it chime softly inside the flat, though no one came to the door. After a couple of minutes, he rang at the next flat along, and got an answer almost at once. The

23

door was opened by an oldish woman, who peered at him round the edge of it, one hand gripping the door and the other clutching the towel which was wrapped around her hair.

'Well?' she asked.

'I'm sorry to have disturbed you,' he began, then paused, as the woman continued to stare blankly at him.

From the direction of the stairs he heard the sound of stealthy footsteps.

The woman flicked one corner of the towel, mopping up a rivulet of water which was running down her neck. 'Tell me what you want, and be quick about it,' she said sharply. 'If you're selling something, the answer's no.'

The footsteps had stopped now, and from the corner of his eye Rawson could see a man, standing quite still, looking at him uncertainly.

'I'm looking for Sonia Dixon, the girl in the flat next door,' Rawson said to the woman, speaking softly so that his voice wouldn't carry to the man. 'I wondered if you could tell me where she is?'

'My dear young man,' the woman

answered, frowning, 'do I look the type of person who would know where to find a girl like her?' Without waiting for a reply, she shut the door firmly.

Rawson turned. The man was still looking at him, though it was impossible to tell whether or not he had heard what the woman had said. When he saw that he was being watched he took a scrap of paper from his pocket and began to study it intently. Rawson walked towards him, slowly. The man crammed the paper back into his pocket, and swung round, hurrying back down the stairs.

Rawson went after him, and the two sets of footsteps clattered wildly on the stone steps. The women with the prams were still at the bottom; the man pushed past them before they had a chance to move. Rawson reached them. One of them looked at him, lips compressed, eyes hard. As he hurried up she thrust her pram at him. It contained a bundle of washing; he staggered into it, half tripped, and fell heavily.

The other woman said: 'That'll teach you a few more manners.'

By the time he was on his feet again, the running man had vanished.

* * *

In a building a few miles away, Philip Roxy twisted his lips nervously. He was a small, dapper man, who, in ten years or so, would be fat; now, he was merely plumpish. He took a pace back and leaned against the wall; it was grimy, and the paint was blistered in parts.

Roxy combined several businesses, but he only just managed to scrape a living. At the front of the building, facing on to the street, was his studio. He would do any photographs which were commissioned, whether there or outside, but, even though his charges were much lower than other photographers, not many people came to him.

He also sold cameras, from a shop which was reached through a door off the studio. He was here now, and facing him across the narrow wooden counter was a much bigger man.

Roxy raised his hand to his thin

moustache, and then he said: 'Well?'

'What do you mean, well?' The other man raised his voice threateningly. 'Have you seen him or haven't you?'

Roxy stared at the man, pressing his lips together. 'I've already told you,' he said smoothly, 'that your brother came round here yesterday. He wanted to talk about the deal over those cameras. I satisfied him and he went away. That's the last I saw of him.'

'And what did Blackie tell you about the deal?'

Now, Roxy ran his tongue over his lips. 'That you wanted the rest of the cash,' he muttered. 'I'd let you have it right away, but — '

'But nothing!' The man stepped back from the counter, measured the distance to the lifting flap which gave access to Roxy's side of it, then kicked out. The flap crashed open and the man stepped behind the counter.

Roxy's smoothness turned to fear. He moved away from the wall and raised his hands as if to protect himself.

'Listen, Harry,' he said, gabbling the

words, 'you'll get your money. It's just that — '

'Listen to me, Phil,' the man named Harry said softly. He made no attempt to go nearer to Roxy, merely stood where he was, his hands at his side.

'Well?'

'When I first realised how easy it would be to hi-jack that lorryload of cameras, I also knew I'd need an outlet. I picked on you because you have the ideal set-up here. You already deal in cameras, you sell to the public and to the trade and you've plenty of contacts. No one's going to worry too much if you suddenly have a few to dispose of cheap.'

'A few!' Roxy cried. 'Do you know how many — '

'Use your contacts,' Harry broke in roughly. 'Use some of these guys you're blackmailing.'

'Now listen — ' Roxy broke off. The main part of his income came from a line of blackmail he ran. He knew that Harry was aware of this, and he also knew that he would be likely to give him away to the cops if he thought it would help. From the first time he had met Harry, one night in a near-by pub, he had realised that he was completely ruthless. He hadn't bothered much then, but now the thought came back into his mind and he shuddered.

Harry said: 'I made a few enquiries and you seemed the ideal bloke. Because you hadn't much capital we agreed that you could pay me half the cash when you got the cameras, and half when you'd got rid of some of them. I know you've sold some, Phil. I want the rest of the dough. That's why I sent Blackie round to see you.'

Blackie was Harry's younger brother, a hard-faced kid who always dressed in a black leather jacket and black jeans.

'Blackie came yesterday,' Roxy said. 'I explained it to him. The cops have sent a letter round to everyone about these cameras. It isn't as easy to get rid of them as it could be, I have to be very careful.' His voice took on a whining note. 'You wouldn't want the cops asking me questions, would you, Harry?'

'What did Blackie say?'

'He agreed with what I'd told him. I said you could have the rest of the money next week. He went away, and I haven't seen him since.'

Harry stared at him. A thought seemed to occur to him. 'Does that deadbeat who works for you know anything about this?'

'Dick Norden? Not a thing,' Roxy assured him hastily. 'He's out now. My receptionist, Miss Woods, is downstairs, but she doesn't know anything either.'

'Keep it that way, Phil. Just find my money and we'll all be pals.' He turned and went towards the door. 'I'll call you this evening.'

He opened the door, and as he went out he chuckled. The sound seemed to Roxy to be evil and sinister.

★ ★ ★

Rawson arrived back at the studio at half past four, to find Janet leafing through a pile of trade magazines. She put down the one in her hand when she saw him come in.

'Anything important?' he asked.

She shook her head. 'There's nothing from Sonia, if that's what you mean. Was there anything at the flat?'

He shook his head, flopping down wearily into one of the black leather chairs. 'Only a bloke keeping an eye on it. I tried to grab him but he was too fast for me.' Better to tell her that than to say that a woman with a pramful of dirty washing had tripped him up. 'The only advantage we've got is that when he saw me I was at the flat next door to Sonia's. He can't be really certain that it was actually Sonia I wanted.'

'But he can guess, if you chased him.'

He shrugged. 'At least he doesn't know who I am, or what I wanted.'

Janet pursed her lips. 'I don't see how that helps us.'

'Neither do I at the moment.' He smoothed down his hair with one hand, and felt anger rising inside him. 'Damn it, Jan, I don't know what to think. Look, do you think we ought to go to the police?'

Janet didn't answer immediately. When she did, she said:

'Are you sure she's really missing?'

'Where else could she be?' he demanded.

'She could have gone away somewhere of her own accord.'

He shook his head. 'You know as well as I do how important she thinks this contract is. Even if she really had to go away, and couldn't put it off, she'd tell me. In any case, who's this character at the flat?'

That was the one inescapable fact that showed that there was something more to this than the fact that Sonia might have been called somewhere urgently.

Janet didn't speak.

Rawson said: 'I did have an idea in the car when I was coming back from Chelsea.'

'What's that?'

'Do you think Philip Roxy could have had anything to do with this?'

'What makes you suggest that?'

'Lots of reasons.' He stood up and began to pace the room, not as an aid to thought but because he felt that he had to do something, make some kind of movement, or he would go mad. 'Roxy thinks that he loves her,' he went on, 'and we know she hates him. To someone with his mind that's as good a reason as any for holding her. Another thing. He wanted this contract with Wesloe's. He might have some idea in his mind that if he — '

'Brian,' Janet broke in softly, 'you're being farfetched. If you ask me, Sonia would have told you if she'd been going there.'

'She might not. She could have guessed that I'd kick up a fuss.' He leaned over the desk so that he could reach the phone book which was kept on the shelf beneath it. 'Do no harm to give him a call and see what he's got to say.'

'And of course he'll tell you all about it.' The sarcasm was strong in Janet's voice. 'If she is there, the only way you'll find out is by going round and asking him, and actually seeing what his reaction is. You won't find out a thing just by phoning him.'

She leaned back, challenging him with her eyes.

He stared at her, then irrationally he remembered what Bill had been saying earlier in the day, and casually ran his eye over her. There was nothing wrong with her figure; if she'd been anyone but his receptionist he'd have jumped at the chance of getting her in front of the camera. Perhaps when this business was all over —

With an effort he switched his thoughts back to Philip Roxy.

'I suppose that if anyone goes round, it should be the police,' he said. 'It isn't up to me to do anything.'

'Possibly not.' Janet's voice was non-committal.

Rawson stood uncertainly, considering what would be the best plan. Silence fell for a second or two, then it was broken by the sound of someone coming up the stairs. The footsteps had started normally, but gradually their speed increased, until the person must have been nearly running. Rawson was reminded vividly of the man he had seen at the flat, then the door was flung open and the person burst into the room.

She stood looking round, breathing hard, then went up to Rawson.

'Mr. Rawson,' she began before he could speak, then stopped and gulped breathlessly. 'Mr. Rawson, you've got to help me.'

4

Request for Help

The girl looked from Rawson to Janet. Her face was flushed from running, and dark hair strayed over it. She brushed away the strands as Rawson took hold of her arm and led her over to one of the chairs. He sat her down, then looked at Janet.

'Any chance of some tea, Jan?' he asked, his eye glinting. Janet should have left for home a couple of minutes ago; she looked glad of this excuse to stay and see what was going on.

While she busied herself with the tea things, Rawson looked at the girl.

She was regaining her breath now, and as her face became calmer and less strained he noticed a strong likeness to Sonia. There was the same oval face, the flesh just full enough to take away any sharp effect without making her look fat, the same straight nose, the same restless energy.

She wore a pale blue coat which fastened with a belt and a single button, no hat, and had short, gently curling, dark hair. She said: 'I'm Sonia Dixon's sister. I've come to you because I know you're a friend of hers, and I need some help.'

'In what way?'

The girl swallowed, and he noticed that her fingers were tightly clenched, the knuckles white.

'There's a man watching the flat,' she said. 'He was there yesterday and he came back again this morning. He followed me for most of the day. Sonia hasn't been home since she left to come here yesterday, and I'm so worried about what might have happened to her.'

Rawson said: 'Maybe she's just gone away for some reason.' There was no need to tell her of his own fears, and it would be interesting to see what she had to say to this.

Before she could answer, Janet came back, with three cups of tea on a tray. She gave one to the girl, who took the cup and the saucer in one hand, keeping the other tightly clenched; Rawson heard a slight rattle, which vanished when she steadied the saucer against her knee.

Her nerves were very bad, that was certain.

She took a sip of the tea, and accepted a biscuit from Janet.

'Sonia hasn't gone away on her own!' she burst out suddenly.

'Certain?'

'She'd have told me, or phoned me, if she had,' the girl declared emphatically.

Rawson nodded. 'Suppose you start at the beginning. We don't even know your name.'

'It's Jean Dixon.' She hesitated, as if she didn't know how to start her story.

'Is the man following you now?' Rawson asked.

She shook her head; the movement almost spilled the tea in her lap. 'I managed to give him the slip on Oxford Street before I came here.'

'How long ago was that?'

'Sometime during the afternoon. I'm not sure exactly when it was.'

Rawson nodded. So the man had been following Jean, lost her, and gone back to the flat to try to find her again. That must have been why he was watching the flat.

He asked: 'Have you been to the police?'

'Not yet.' Jean bit her lip. 'I did think of it, but it seems such a silly thing to go to them with. I mean, there's not much I can tell them.'

'So you came to me because I was the next best thing?' He smiled, trying to put the girl more at her ease, but she continued to stare at him. 'You were the only person I could think of,' she said at length. 'Even though Sonia's so well known, we haven't many friends. I knew that you were a friend of hers, though, because she often mentioned you, and I thought — ' She broke off, and managed a weak smile.

'And you've no idea at all where she could be?'

'None at all. I've phoned a few places where she might have gone, but she isn't at any of them. If she were anywhere else, I'm sure she'd have let me know.'

'You don't know of anyone who might want to kidnap her?' he asked mildly, with a glance at Janet.

The question didn't seem to surprise Jean. She thought for a minute, then answered: 'No one at all unless it's that chap she had the row with, Roxy, or whatever he's called.'

'I thought she wasn't going to see Roxy again?'

'She wasn't — not to work, that is — but she did have one or two things to clear up with him. I know that she was thinking of going there yesterday afternoon if she had the time.'

Rawson grabbed up the phone book again. He found Roxy's number, dialled it and hung up when there was no answer.

'Look, Jean,' he said, coming to a sudden decision, 'let me take you back to your flat. There's every chance of that bloke turning up there again, but he can't stop there for ever. When he leaves, I'll follow him, and we'll see where he goes. Once we know that, we can decide what to do about calling in the police.'

Jean stood up quickly, putting the

empty cup back on the tray. Her hand didn't tremble as she reached out for the door knob.

No one followed them to the flat.

★　★　★

It was a dolly flat, and everywhere was evidence of Sonia's considerable income. Once past the pale pinkness of the corridor, a small square hall led into the living-room with two doors opening off this which would lead to kitchen and bedroom. All the woodwork was finished in white gloss, with pale cream paper on the walls. A painting done entirely in straight lines hung on the wall with the two doors in it, while from alongside the black settee a four-foot-high woolly poodle gazed at him blankly.

Jean crossed to the large window and looked down into the street.

'I can't see him yet,' she said. 'He normally waits by that newsagent's on the opposite corner.'

Rawson sat down on the settee while Jean poured drinks. He ran his hand over the poodle's back, feeling the simulated fur coarser than he had expected. Jean handed him his drink and sat down next to him. She was wearing a deep blue dress which looked as though it had been made from a shirt which had been a little on the small side; his eyes went to her legs, then he looked away.

She said: 'It's very good of you to go to all this trouble, Brian.'

'I shouldn't worry about that.' He grinned at her. 'Let's say that the Wesloe contract gives me a professional interest.'

She managed a laugh. 'I almost hope that bloke does come back. If he stays away now, you'll think I've brought you on a wild-goose chase.'

'And haven't you?' There was no need, yet, to tell her that he had already seen the man.

'Of course not!' She spoke a shade crossly, then the mood went as quickly as it had come. 'I'm sorry. I'm not in such a good mood, as you can gather.'

'I don't blame you.' He drank more of the best whisky he had tasted for some time. 'You've no idea who this bloke could be? He couldn't be someone who's threatened you or Sonia in the past, could he?'

'I don't think so. There's probably only Roxy who comes into that category, anyway.'

'Everything comes back to Roxy,' Rawson mused. 'But yet why should this bloke follow you? I think I'll have another go at calling Roxy.'

He put his glass on the floor, straightened up and began to get out of his seat. As he did so, Jean also moved, then turned quickly as there came a faint noise from the door. They collided hard, and Rawson was sent sprawling on the settee, Jean stumbling and falling on top of him. Automatically, to stop her falling further, his arms went round her. He felt her body, soft and warm through the thin material of the dress, and then their lips met.

From the door a voice said: 'What the devil do you think you're doing with my fiancée?'

5

Fiancée

The man who came in as Jean scrambled away from Rawson was about his size but more heavily built, with dark, closely cropped hair that gave him a Germanic appearance. He stood with his feet slightly apart and his fingers curling, gazing at Rawson. Suddenly, he swung to face Jean, who was smoothing her dress.

'So this is what you get up to while I'm away?'

'Mike, listen before you say anything.' Jean sounded completely calm, as if she had the situation fully in hand. 'This is Brian Rawson, the photographer whom Sonia's working with.' She turned to Rawson, 'This is Mike Cartney,' she said to him.

'Where's Sonia?' Cartney demanded.

'That's why Brian's here. She's vanished, there's a man following me, and because I didn't expect you back until the end of the week I went to Brian for help.'

She paused. Cartney, breathing hard, looked from her to Rawson.

'I can see you didn't expect me back,' he observed. 'I suppose Rawson's named a price for his help?'

Rawson raised his eyebrows. 'Jean and I got up at the same time. We collided. That's all there is to it.'

Cartney frowned and then said: 'What do you mean, Sonia's disappeared?'

'I mean that she should have come to my place today and she didn't turn up,' Rawson snapped, suddenly angry. 'It was for an important contract we're working on and I can't think of anything that would have kept her away.'

Jean asked: 'Mike, did you see anyone outside when you came in?'

Cartney stepped farther into the room. All the time he had been standing there, the door to the passage had been open; he shut it now, then spoke heavily. 'There was a smallish chap wearing a brown raincoat standing outside that news-agent's across the road. To tell you the truth, I didn't take much notice of him.'

Jean crossed to the window, Rawson close behind her.

'That's the man,' she said as she looked out. 'What are we going to do now?'

Rawson saw the man he had chased earlier in the day.

Cartney said: 'I don't know what you and I are going to do, Jeannie, but Rawson is going to get back to his studio.'

'Why?' Rawson asked mildly.

'Because this is no concern of yours now,' Cartney answered rudely. 'I'm grateful for whatever you were going to do, but I'm here now. I'll look after Jean.'

Rawson took a deep breath. He wanted to argue, but if he did Jean would feel bound to support him, and he didn't want to cause any more friction between her and Cartney.

Cartney came closer to him. 'If you're so bothered about it, why don't you get the police?'

'Look,' Rawson said, 'there's no point in standing here arguing, is there?'

Cartney pressed his lips together.

'Mike,' Jean said, grabbing his arm as if

46

to restrain him, 'it's my sister who's disappeared, and I'm the one who might be in danger next.'

'But — '

'Mike,' Jean said very quietly, 'either you can be a bit more reasonable, or you can get out.'

Cartney frowned at her, then moved abruptly to the settee and threw himself down on it. 'All right, Rawson, let's hear what you've got against the police.'

Rawson sat in one of the easy chairs, while Jean sat on the settee, close to Cartney. Rawson wondered fleetingly just what the relationship between them was; Cartney had his own key and was supposedly engaged to Jean, yet there was a coldness between them which certainly shouldn't have been there. He put that out of his mind for the moment and said:

'I haven't got anything against the police, but I think that this is something we can do better than they can.'

'In what way?' The sneer was still in Cartney's voice, although he spoke more softly.

'What would happen if we rang them

now? They'd send someone round and our friend across the road would see him and scarper. There's no reason to arrest him, but even if they did he'd only have to deny everything and they'd have to let him go. We'd have got rid of him but we wouldn't be any nearer finding out what he's after, and by tomorrow there'd be someone else.'

Cartney leaned forward, his hands clasped round one knee. 'So what do you intend to do?' For the first time there was neither sneer nor anger in his voice, only interest.

'He's got to go home sometime,' Rawson answered. 'I'm going to wait here, and when he goes I'll follow him. If I think it's serious enough after that, I'll call the police.' He sat back to watch the effect of his closely reasoned argument.

Cartney spoke to Jean. 'Do you agree with him?'

She nodded.

Cartney grunted, pulling one leg off the floor with his clasped hands. 'I suppose you might have something,' he conceded. 'We'd better take it in turns to watch the window. I'll have first go, then we'll do half-hour spells.'

He stood up and moved one of the small chairs over to the window, placing it carefully so that he could see out without being too noticeable from the road.

Jean said: 'I didn't expect you back so soon.'

For the first time since he had come in Cartney grinned. 'So I gather. I finished my business earlier than I expected, and I thought it'd surprise you if I came here tonight . . . '

The evening passed slowly, the atmosphere still slightly strained. It was a few minutes aften ten when the man left, the suddenness of his decision taking them all by surprise. Rawson rushed across the room, fearful that he would lose him after waiting so long. When he reached the street, the man was still in sight, although he was so far away that his thin form was almost invisible in the darkness. Rawson wondered whether or not to take his car, which he had left in a near-by alley, then decided not to. The man was walking, and a car would only be a hindrance.

He followed him quickly, closing up the distance as much as he dared. The man walked at a surprisingly fast pace until he came to Fulham tube station. He paused then, looking round him as if he wasn't quite certain where he was. Rawson waited some distance away, shivering in the chill of the night and wishing that he had brought an overcoat. Eventually, the man made up his mind which way to go and walked on briskly. He turned a corner, and was out of sight for a moment or two. There came the sound of a motorcycle engine, and with a sudden sharp feeling of horror Rawson ran the rest of the way to the corner.

He had been right.

He was just in time to see the tail light fading away, and there was no sign of the man he had been following.

* * *

It was almost midnight when he arrived back at his flat. He had been to Chelsea, merely to collect his car, as he didn't see the point of calling at the flat at that time of night just to confess failure. He felt certain that they wouldn't expect anything from him until morning, and he might have come up with some other ideas by then. He drove the car back with a savage burst of speed, garaged it, then ran up the stairs into the reception room.

He switched on the lights, glanced round to make sure that everything was in order, then went on to his flat, just along the corridor. He had fitted out the building like that because he often worked odd hours and it was an advantage not to have to drive home after a long and tiring spell.

Though not as luxurious as Sonia's flat, it was a snug and comfortable home. In the living-room, two chairs covered in a deep red leather stood before an electric fire. A television set was in one corner, flanked by a low table and magazine rack. He crossed the room and went into the kitchen.

Nothing at all had been disturbed.

He wondered whether or not to ring Jean. There were one or two odd things about Cartney to bear in mind, and he was there with her on his own. He had turned up unexpectedly at just the right moment. He had been against Rawson's presence. He could easily be involved himself.

The phone rang shrilly, interrupting his thoughts.

This was an extension of the one on Janet's desk and could either be switched through to the flat or the reception room. Suddenly cautious, he picked up the receiver.

'Rawson.'

He heard Cartney's voice.

'I think you ought to know this, Rawson. We've just had someone here, asking if we know where Sonia is.'

'Who is he?' Rawson demanded.

There was a pause before Cartney spoke, in a harsh voice.

'He was a copper, Rawson.'

6

A Copper Calls

'Are you sure he was actually a policeman?' Rawson asked after a moment, 'and not just someone with a faked warrant card?'

'He was wearing a uniform.'

'It's more difficult to fake a uniform, I agree.' He wanted time to think. 'Whatever they want her for can't be too serious, or they would have sent more than one man, or a plain-clothes man, at least.'

Cartney hesitated before answering. Finally, he asked: 'Just what is Sonia to you?'

'What do you mean?'

Again the hesitancy, then: 'Well, to put it bluntly, is she just a clothes horse or is she something a little more than that?'

'Haven't you asked Jean?'

'I'm asking you.'

'We were supposed to have been going out this evening,' Rawson told him slowly. 'We had something to celebrate. Anything could have happened after that. You know how it is.'

Cartney grunted. 'Changed your mind about going to the cops?'

'It looks as though they've come to us. What did you tell this character?'

'That she was out, and we didn't know where she was.'

Rawson smiled faintly. It must have taken a lot of effort for Cartney to say that; he wondered whether Jean had had anything to do with it.

Cartney was speaking again: 'What happened to that bloke you were following?'

'I lost him.'

'Lost him! Christ! What do you propose we do now?'

'I'm not really sure,' Rawson said. 'We could wait until tomorrow, and try to pick him up again, I suppose.'

Cartney's voice was suddenly harsh over the wire. 'Listen, Rawson, this may be just a caper to you, but I want you to bear one thing in mind. You said yourself that there could be some danger to Jean. If anything happens to her while you're pussyfooting around like this, there'll be trouble. There'll be more trouble if anything's happened to Sonia. Got that?'

'I've got it,' Rawson answered. He banged down the phone and turned away, suddenly weary. While he had been following the thin man an idea had come into his mind, and he had forced it away because he had no proof, and he didn't want to believe it anyway. It returned now, stranger than before.

The thin man could represent some kind of gang. If that were the case he could be looking for Sonia because she had been involved with some kind of racket. If the police were also looking for her, without having been told that she was missing, that theory was strengthened.

He crossed to a chair and sat down. It looked pretty much as though Cartney would give the police all the help he could from now on; he had stalled the man tonight, but the police were persistent devils once they started and they would be back at Sonia's in force very soon. He managed a weak smile at the pun in his thoughts, then began to try to decide what to do.

It was unlikely that Sonia was involved in a racket, but not impossible.

There was the load of stolen Minolta cameras she had mentioned to him before, to start with. A model who mixed with the wrong set could easily be involved in something like that.

But, Sonia hadn't been mixing with the wrong set. The only photographer he knew who might be involved was Roxy.

He yawned, and stood up. In spite of the time, he was going to see Roxy.

★ ★ ★

Even though he had heard so much about Roxy he had never been to his place before. He had had to look up the address in the phone book, and had almost rang him to say that he was coming. He had changed his mind as soon as he had picked up the receiver; why warn him when the sole purpose of the visit was to catch him unawares?

At that time of night, there was no traffic about at all, and the Triumph made good time as far as Shaftesbury Avenue. Roxy's studio was in a little side street off here, and Rawson had to look for it. He managed to find it at last, but it was narrower than he had thought, and had it not been on his side of the road he would almost certainly have missed it. As it was, he had to brake sharply and reverse a few yards before he could make the turn.

He saw the illuminated sign farther along: 'Roxy's Studio'.

He stopped the car, blocking the alley, intent on the sign, then drove a few yards farther along. Here, some buildings had been knocked down and he could pull the car off the road and leave room for other traffic to get past — if there was any.

He got out and went over to the studio. It was a flashy place, with none of the quiet elegance which was found at most good photographers. The neon sign glared above the door, the shop front showed yellow in the glow from the single street lamp, and the door seemed to be purple. A number of framed prints were in the window, and he saw one of Sonia. Her hair was hanging to her shoulders, slightly disarrayed, and the expression on her face gave her the wild, almost gypsy look, which came out in so many of her pictures. Somehow, though, the picture was flat and lifeless, and the look that should have been in her eyes, the sparkle, was missing.

He thought: If she knew that was there, she'd make him take it out.

Somehow, the fact that it was there gave a reassurance that she probably hadn't been anywhere near the place.

He rang the illuminated bell at the side of the door, trying again when no one answered him. There was still no answer. On trying the door, he found it open, and he stepped inside cautiously.

'Roxy!' he called softly.

There was no answer. He went farther into the shop, letting the door swing shut behind him. As his eyes became accustomed to the gloom he could make out another door on the far side of the room, and a desk with a sinister-looking hooded typewriter squatting on it. Crossing to this door he opened it, and went up the flight of stairs behind it.

He assumed they would lead to the camera room and the rest of the studio. The entry in the phone book had shown no private address, so he had assumed that Roxy lived here, just as he lived at his studio. If he didn't, that would explain the silence, but it wouldn't explain everything.

It wouldn't explain the open door.

He tried a door at the top of the stairs. It opened on to a small room with a long mirror and a white enamel sink which gleamed in the darkness. It was obviously a dressing-room. He shut the door and tried another one.

This was better. It lead into the camera room. In the moonlight which came in through a small window at one end he could just make out the camera, still set up on a tripod, a large wooden trunk near it, and a long bench down the side. A light switch was by his hand; he pressed it down, and saw the rest of the things in the room.

A body sprawled in front of the bench, a knife still in its ribs, bloodstains on the floor.

In the midst of all the blood was a girl's black shoe, with the letter 'S' picked out in white on the toe. One of Sonia's shoes.

After standing by the door for a moment, he moved forward. It was easy to assume that the dead man was Philip Roxy; there was little doubt about it, and proof would be difficult without touching the body. He remembered a photo of Roxy that had once appeared in the trade press, that of a small, almost dapper man, with a moustache. The description fitted.

He stared down. There were two things he could do. One, the easiest one, was to go away as quietly as he had come, and let someone else find the body in the morning. The snag there was that someone might have seen him come, and in any event his car was parked near by and there was no telling who had seen that. A passing copper could have noticed it, for instance, and remembered it because of the lateness of the hour. If he went away now and it was proved later that he had been here, he would be in trouble.

It would be better to call the police.

There was still Sonia's shoe to think about.

Nerving himself, and trying to control his breath, which was coming in short gasps, he reached out to touch the dead man's forehead. It was still warm. Whoever had killed him had done so very recently, so recently that he might still be here, roaming round the other rooms. Rawson felt a prickle of fear on his scalp, then he reached out carefully and picked the shoe up, holding it by the edge of the sole so that he would leave no fingerprints on it. He had last seen it only the day before, when Sonia had been wearing that pair at the studio. The obvious reasoning was that she had been here and killed Roxy, but there were still problems.

Roxy had died recently. If Sonia had killed him, where had she been until now? More important, if she had killed him and lost her shoe, she was now walking around with only one shoe on. Yet, if she hadn't killed Roxy, or been present at the murder, how had her shoe got there?

As he stood up, still holding the shoe in his right hand, he heard the doorbell peal. For a moment, the significance of the sound didn't penetrate his mind; when it did his first thought was that the police were here. His breath rasped and panic came into his mind, then he realised that there was no reason for the police to call, unless the killer had sent them. That was hardly likely, but the only other answer was that it was some friend of Roxy's, who had arranged to call, and who would be expecting an answer to his ring

Quickly, he went out of the camera room into the reception room, where he pushed the shoe under the typewriter cover, then looked towards the door. Through the glass part of it he could see a shadow of a man standing outside. His arm moved, and the bell shrilled again. Rawson stepped to the door and opened it carefully, letting it hide him as it swung back.

The man stepped inside, pausing when he saw no one.

'Strewth, mate, where are you?' he asked loudly. He moved forward, and Rawson saw him clearly.

It was the thin man who had been following Jean.

7

Thin Man

Rawson said: 'I'm right behind you.'

He shut the door with his foot, and the man spun round, making a funny whistling sound through his teeth.

'Strewth, mate, you startled me,' he said. 'Where's the boss?'

'You mean Roxy?'

'You should know who the boss is.'

Rawson said: 'Roxy's dead.'

'Dead?'

The man had been walking towards the back of the room, as if he had intended to go up the stairs. He paused with one hand on the door knob, and a sudden trace of fear showed in his eyes. He had the look of a man who has butted in on something and wishes he hadn't. He made the whistling noise again then started towards Rawson, his hands hanging at his sides, his fingers curling.

'You've killed him,' he said softly, all trace of fear gone now.

'I didn't kill him.' Rawson stayed where he was until the thin man was right up to him. 'Why should I want to kill him?'

'Because you both fancy the bird in the pictures and you think he had more of a chance with her than you have.'

There was no time to wonder what the man meant, which bird and which pictures he was referring to, as in another moment any advantage that Rawson might have now would be gone.

He reached out, catching the man's coat and pulling him forward. As he stumbled, Rawson stepped to one side, putting out his foot. The man tripped and staggered across the room. His hands slapped against the wall as he saved himself from falling, then Rawson grabbed him again, gripping one arm and twisting it up his back. The man gave a faint moan. By pulling on the twisted arm Rawson forced him across the room and into the chair behind the desk. He noticed some light switches on the wall;

crossing to them he put on the room lights.

The man was rubbing his arm.

Rawson said: 'Which bird am I supposed to fancy?'

'You should know,' the man muttered sullenly.

Rawson tried a different line. 'What are you doing here at this time?'

'Who the hell are you?' The man stopped rubbing his arm and glared at him.

Rawson smiled faintly. 'Let's say that I'm the man who didn't kill Roxy.'

'Then if you didn't kill him, who did?'

'That's what I'm trying to find out. What's your name?' He added the last question in such a sharp voice that the man was taken aback.

'Bradford,' he blurted.

'And what are you doing here?' Still the sharp voice.

'I came to tell Roxy about the job.'

'Listen, Bradford, don't be funny.' Awareness of his own position pushed Rawson on. He was known to be friendly with Sonia, and through that he could be shown to have reason for quarrelling with Roxy. If the police came now, Bradford would say that he had found Rawson with the body, and that would be the end of any serious police effort to find anyone else who could have killed him. Whatever else happened, he had to get something out of Bradford before the lights and the car outside attracted someone's attention. Sweat broke out on his forehead as he realised how much the bright lights would stand out in the dark street, but it was too late to do anything about it now.

'What job?' he asked Bradford.

Bradford swallowed. 'Roxy asked me to follow a bird. I came to tell him what happened. I was going to leave it till morning, then I remembered that he'd asked me to come tonight and said he wouldn't pay me if I didn't do what I was told. So I came round.'

'And which bird am I supposed to fancy?'

Bradford shifted in his seat so that he could reach his pockets. He took out two slightly crumpled photos and passed them to Rawson. He took them, keeping one eye on the man as he did so. One of them was a picture of Jean Dixon, taken in the street when she wouldn't know anything about it, and obviously given to Bradford so that he would recognise her.

The other was a colour photo of Sonia, naked on a bed, one knee raised carefully.

He dropped them on the desk. Bradford licked his lips as though he were going to ask for them back, then changed his mind.

'Did Roxy give you those?'

He nodded.

'Listen, Bradford,' Rawson said, 'someone killed Roxy earlier this evening. It wasn't me, but the police are going to pick on me. I don't care what I do to get the truth, so I suggest you tell me everything that you know.'

Bradford licked his lips. 'Roxy'll kill me — ' he began, then stopped.

'Roxy won't do anything.'

Bradford hesitated, then started to speak, the words coming in a fast gabble. 'I've done one or two jobs for Roxy before. I didn't think anything of it when he rang me up and told me he wanted someone followed. I came round here and he gave me the pictures.'

'Both of them?'

'Just the one in the street.'

'What about the other?'

'I — I picked it up when he wasn't looking. She looked a bit of all right, and I thought he'd have plenty more.' He ran his tongue over his lips and moved his arm as though to fend off an attack. 'Honest, mate, I didn't mean no harm, I — '

'Get on with it.'

Bradford swallowed. 'I followed the girl, like he said, that one in the street. He wanted to know where she went, if she went to the cops or to another photographer, a bloke called Rawson. It all figured to me. Rawson had been messing about with this bird, Roxy had found out and was putting the black on by threatening to tell Rawson's wife.'

'Or the girl's husband,' Rawson said mildly.

'Could be, mate.'

'And how would you recognise Rawson? Would you have a photo of him?'

He spoke quickly, trying to hurry up the questioning, still horribly conscious of the glaring lights, yet aware that to put them out would make it simple for Bradford to get away.

'No picture, mate,' Bradford was saying. 'Roxy said that when I told him the places she'd been to he'd know if Rawson's was among them.'

'And did she go there?'

'She might have done.' Bradford's voice was suddenly harsh. 'She gave me the slip, the first time anyone's done that for years. 'Course, I had to tell Roxy and he said to go back to the flat and try and pick her up later. If nothing happened by ten o'clock, to report here. That's the lot.'

Rawson sensed that he was keeping something back, but he wasn't given a chance to wonder what it was, for Bradford spoke again.

'I fancy Rawson for the killing, mate. If he found out that Roxy was putting the black on him or his bird, he could kill him.'

'Roxy did a lot of blackmailing?'

Bradford nodded. He glanced casually

to one corner of the room, and Rawson's eyes were drawn after his.

Bradford sprang from the chair and charged him. He hit him with his shoulder, unbalancing him and sending him sliding along the floor. The phone crashed to the floor, making a tinging sound, but not breaking.

Bradford was racing towards the door. He reached it and his fingers scrabbled at the handle, slipping off it before he had turned it. He looked back at Rawson, who was now on his knees, then licked his lips and pulled at the door again.

It opened.

He almost tripped over it in his hurry to get out, crashed it back, and ran. Rawson ran after him. The door was swinging back gently after Bradford had banged it open, and he was held up fractionally while he opened it again.

One thought was uppermost in his mind. Now that Roxy was dead, Bradford was the only man who might know where Sonia was. He had to catch him, had to carry on questioning him until he was certain that he had nothing more to tell.

By the time he reached the street, the man was about fifty yards away, still running, and glancing over his shoulder. There was almost no one else about; except for the two running men and a drunk swaying crazily round the lamp-post at the end of the street, it was empty. Soon, Bradford would reach Shaftesbury Avenue, where he could easily pick up a taxi, or where he might have left his motorbike.

Suddenly, a dark-coloured van swung into the street, the sound of its engine carrying clearly on the night air. The drunk made another circuit of the lamp-post, then waved to the van driver, shouting something as he did so.

The van's headlamps came on, picking out Bradford and holding him. Bradford ran. The van swung on to the pavement. Bradford's scream was cut off sharply as it hit him and flung him into the air. He landed in front of it, and it bounced over him and then sped on.

It was heading straight for Rawson.

8

Murder by Van

The van was moving very fast.

Rawson had more chance of avoiding it than Bradford had had, if only because he knew the van driver's intentions. As it had swerved on to the pavement earlier, he had stopped running, and now he stood in its path, undecided what to do. By his side was a shallow doorway; it wasn't very deep, but it might just keep him away from the van.

He crammed himself into it.

The roar of the van's engine filled his ears. He felt it rush past, felt the door handle catch in the material of his jacket, tearing the cloth and almost pulling him out of the doorway, then it was gone. He stepped out of his shelter, and nearly fell as reaction set in and his legs began to tremble. He leaned against the wall, clutching a drainpipe, trying to force

73

himself to go on, towards the dark blob which was Bradford's body.

The drunk stared down the street. Suddenly, he let go of the lamp-post, staggered round in a semi-circle, and lurched off towards the main road. Rawson watched him, tested his own legs, and found them still weak. He tried to go towards the body, changed his mind, and started back towards the studio. As he walked, his mind began to clear again; by the time he reached the door he was able to walk fairly normally. He tried to recall the details of the van, but he recalled seeing no number plate and nothing but a blur where the driver was sitting.

He knew that he would never recognise either the van or its driver again.

Whoever he was, he had almost certainly killed Roxy, too.

He went into the studio, knowing that he would have to call the police now. Of course, if he showed them the body and the shoe, they would assume that Sonia had killed him. If he didn't show them the shoe, they were likely to think he had killed him. Somehow, he would have to explain why he had come here at this time of night, without involving Sonia.

He crossed to the desk, picked up the phone from the floor and replaced it; there was still a dialling tone, so it wasn't broken. Reaching under the typewriter cover, he took out the shoe. He hurried out to his car, slipped it into the glove compartment, then returned to the studio.

He called the police.

They arrived soon afterwards, a man with a camera, another, taller man who looked like a doctor and a man who seemed to be in charge but who looked to Rawson as if he wasn't tall enough to be a policeman.

'Good evening, sir,' this man said. 'I'm Chief Superintendent Heaton.'

He had a rumpled look about him, as if he had just got out of bed; he didn't offer to shake hands, but after telling Rawson to stay where he was he bustled about, organising everything. More men arrived. Heaton did some more bustling, arranging the setting up of flood-lamps around the dead Bradford, then when everything was done to his satisfaction, he came over to Rawson, sat down in the chair Bradford had used, and folded his arms.

When Heaton had first joined the force he had only just cleared the height regulations, and now the fact that he was nearly always in the company of exceptionally tall people made him look smaller than he actually was. There had been jokes about his height at one time, but his rapid promotion had stopped that.

'Now, Mr. Rawson,' he began, 'tell me exactly what you've seen, and what you're doing here at this time in the morning.'

Rawson hesitated, collecting his thoughts, then gave a brief summary of the facts, which was taken down by a uniformed man sitting behind Heaton. He didn't mention Sonia, but started from the time Jean had arrived at his studio.

When he had finished, Heaton pursed his lips. 'Any idea why this man Bradford should have been following the girl, or why Roxy should have wanted her followed?'

'No. That's what I came here to find out.'

'Why here, particularly? Did you know that Roxy was at the back of it?'

'I didn't actually know,' Rawson said carefully, 'but it was easy enough to guess. He'd been making a bit of a nuisance of himself lately, ringing her up, trying to get her at home, that sort of thing.'

He lied easily. He mustn't mention Sonia, mustn't let him know that she had been here, at least, until he had had a chance to look for himself and see how much she was involved. Once he had decided to leave her out, it was remarkable how well the story hung together. Jean Dixon had come to his studio. She was a girl he knew slightly, through friends, and she had told him that a man was following her. Roxy's name had been mentioned, and although Rawson was busy at the time he had promised her that he would call round to see Roxy as soon as he could and see what he had to say. He had found him dead. The man who had been following Jean had come to report to his boss;

minutes later, he had been knocked down by a van.

That was all.

'Don't suppose you got the number of the van?' Heaton asked, without much hope in his voice.

Rawson shook his head. 'All I was worried about was saving myself.'

'Reasonable enough. Did you disturb anything here?'

Rawson hesitated. 'No,' he said eventually.

'So we can take it that everything is as the killer left it?'

'In the studio, yes. I had a bit of a scuffle with Bradford in here and one or two things might have been disturbed.'

Heaton nodded. 'It's more the other room that I'm concerned about. You'll realise how important it is that I see that just as it was left.'

Rawson looked at him. Was it imagination or was Heaton pushing this point slightly too much? He tried to recall whether or not he had left any indications that he had moved the shoe; as far as he could tell, he hadn't, but you could never tell what modern police methods could pick up. For the first time he felt slightly uneasy at the task he had taken on, but he was committed now.

Behind Heaton, the constable was writing swiftly. Heaton himself was looking absently round the room; he stared at some photos for a moment then he said:

'From what you said earlier, I gather that you only knew Miss Jean Dixon slightly, through some friends of yours?'

'That's right.'

'Then why should she come to you? Surely she had friends of her own, people whom she knew better than she knew you? Wouldn't she be more likely to go to them?'

This was a weak spot in Rawson's story; he had thought of this, and thought that he had a good explanation to cover it.

There was another weak spot, worse, which he hadn't thought of yet.

'Jean came to me because I'm a photographer,' he said easily. 'She reckoned that I might know Roxy and be able to deal with him better than her other friends.'

'What about this boyfriend of hers? Mike Cartney?'

'Apparently she expected him to be away for the rest of the week. He turned up unexpectedly. I suppose that if she'd known he was coming home so soon she'd have waited until he arrived.'

'I see.' Heaton pulled at his lip. 'I'll have to go and see the girl, of course, if you'll let me have a note of her address.'

Rawson's heart lurched. He had overlooked the most obvious thing that was wrong with his story. As soon as the police saw Cartney, he would blow the whole thing wide open, though at least he couldn't tell them about the shoe. As there was no choice, he gave the address of Jean's flat, then said:

'You aren't going round there now, are you? I don't think she'd be very pleased if the police knocked her up at this time.'

'I think we can leave it until tomorrow,' Heaton conceded. 'She probably can't add much to what you've told me. I'd be obliged if you'd sign a typewritten statement, when I've had it done.'

Rawson said: 'Of course.'

He went out.

'Good night, Mr. Rawson,' Heaton called.

★ ★ ★

While Rawson was going home, and Superintendent Heaton, still at Roxy's, was wishing that he could do the same, a man named Harding was saying:

'I got him.'

'I should hope so.'

'There was another character there, Harry. I think it was this Rawson. I nearly got him, too.'

For a few seconds there was a silence in the room. It was an average room, that might be found in any block of flats. A large television set stood in one corner, and near it, on a low table, was a radio set in a polished wooden cabinet. A foreign station was on; a crooner moaned softly in Spanish. Harry was sitting in an armchair; he stared at Harding, then suddenly banged the palm of his hand down on the leather arm.

The sound was like a pistol shot.

'Christ, Frank,' Harry cried, 'have you no sense? We need Rawson now to help us get rid of the cameras.' He stared at the other man, who nodded.

'Bradford's dead, though, and none of Roxy's other contacts know too much about it, so we should be all right. There's only that creep who worked for Roxy.'

Harry smiled. 'Dick Norden? As far as I'm concerned, he doesn't know a thing. Roxy would have had more sense than tell him anything.'

'I wouldn't be too sure.'

Harry waved him to silence. 'Look, Frank, we've got to decide what we're doing now. When it was just a few cameras that had been stolen we weren't so bad, but it's murder now. The cops are going to be out in full strength, and you know what that means.' He stopped and pointed his finger at Harding. 'We'll have to lie low, Frank. We can't stay here, or at Cliff's.' Cliff was Harry's elder brother.

'So what do we do?'

'We'll get on to Simon Collins at

Limehouse. He'll let us have a room that they'll never find.'

Harding nodded.

'The other thing,' Harry went on, 'is that we've got these cameras back on our hands. I was relying on getting rid of them through Roxy's warehouse but that's finished with now. The only other hope is Rawson.' He paused. 'See what I mean about keeping him alive?'

'Think it's safe to have him working for us?'

'I've got all kinds of people working for me,' Harry said airily. 'People you'd never dream of work for me.' His voice became more serious again. 'The only trouble will be with Rawson's girl-friend, Sonia. She's a lot of help to us now, but she might talk afterwards. I guess we'll sort it out, though.'

He grinned, and then began to chuckle softly.

★   ★   ★

In spite of his late night, Rawson was up early the following morning. He lay dozing for a minute or two after the alarm had gone off, then sat up quickly, realising what he had done the night before. If Heaton beat him to Jean's flat, the fact that he had lied to the police would come out, and Heaton would be after him. Quite apart from the danger to Sonia, there were other factors, too, things which he hadn't seen the night before, with his mind fogged by the need to keep Sonia out of it.

It would come out that, while Roxy was actually after Sonia, not Jean, she hated him, and hated him more after the way he pawed her at their last session together. When added to the fact that Rawson had almost taken her out, and that she was known to be fond of him, it would make a good case for the two men hating each other. In addition to all this, Roxy needed business badly. He had put in for the Wesloe contract, and Rawson had got it instead. Not only had he taken the work from him, but it was work which would have meant being with Sonia for long periods.

Could Heaton get a murder case out of that?

And why were the police after Sonia?

Rawson groaned as he realised how complicated the whole business was. He was still convinced in his own mind that Sonia had done nothing criminal; if she had been criminally minded there had been ample opportunity in her career so far to get on faster by being dishonest, and she hadn't fallen for it. There was no reason for her to fall for it now, especially with the Wesloe pictures in the offing.

However you looked at it, things were in a hell of a mess.

He slid out of bed and dressed quickly. The only thing that might help would be getting to Jean's before the police did, and warning her. That would still leave the problem of Cartney, but he felt that once he had explained to him that Sonia might be wanted on a murder charge he would see reason. After that, he intended to look for her himself; it might be a hopeless task, but at least he could try.

He gulped down his breakfast, then

made an attempt at phoning Jean. The line was engaged. He put the phone down, and collected the Triumph from its garage. At this time of the morning the traffic was heavy, but he forced his way through it, helped by the fact that he was driving a sports car. He had left a note for Janet to tell her where he was; she had her own key, so she could open up, and he expected to be back before the first client was due.

He arrived at the flat a little after quarter to nine, and rang the bell. Cartney answered the door. He said nothing, merely held the door wide so that Rawson could enter.

He went in. He saw Jean, sitting on the settee, one hand on the poodle's head as if she were using it for protection from something he couldn't see. She was wearing a white blouse and short, black skirt, with a wide orange V-pleat down the front. Cartney was still wearing the things he had worn the day before, which suggested that he had stayed the night.

He saw Heaton.

Heaton said: 'Good morning, Mr. Rawson, I'm glad you've called round. There are one or two things here that don't quite fit in with what you told me last night.'

9

Action at the Yard

Afterwards, it seemed to Rawson as if Cartney must have told Heaton everything. This was not so; Cartney had had to tell him very little, as most of the information had been obtained through the sharpness of Sergeant Field.

In spite of the fact that it was only eight o'clock when Heaton arrived at the Yard, Field was already at his desk. He was a tall, thin man, though his thinness concealed almost inexhaustible energy. Although he assisted Heaton in most of his cases he had not been at Roxy's the night before, and would know nothing about the murder unless he had read the few lines in the morning paper.

Heaton shut the door of the office, threw his hat on to a peg, as he had been doing every morning for the past seven years, and sat down at his desk. When he had left the night before, the desk had been reasonably clear; now there was a pile of papers and reports on it, and Field was sorting another pile on his own desk.

He pushed the stack to one side.

'Morning, John,' he said to Heaton.

'Morning.' Heaton grunted the greetings, and yawned. 'Anything big in?'

'Not so far.'

That was a good start. He flipped quickly through the stack, saw that he might be able to farm most of them out to others, and gave a slight grin.

'Spot of trouble up Shaftesbury Avenue last night.' He gave Field brief details; the rest could follow when there was more time.

'They called you out?' Field asked, his eyes narrowing.

'That's right.'

'What did Kath have to say?'

Heaton sighed. 'The usual.'

Kath was his wife. She had never quite got used to the odd hours which he had to work as a policeman. When he had had his latest promotion she had been happier for a few weeks, thinking that things might be better at last. In fact, they had gradually worsened; the higher rank meant that he was more liable than ever to be called out at short notice. He pushed away the picture that came into his mind, of Kath sitting up in bed, yawning, her hair fluffed out, as she dragged on the pale pink bed-jacket that he had bought her as a surprise present, and forced himself to concentrate on what Field was saying.

'Why call you out, John? What's the matter with Len Harrow? He's supposed to be on nights for that area, isn't he?'

Heaton yawned again. 'He is, but the people here are convinced that this fits in with that other case I'm working on. You know the one, the missing camera job.'

Field nodded. 'Seems reasonable if it's a photographer.'

'But not so reasonable that I have to be dragged out of bed to go and look at the blighter.' Heaton sat back. 'I wonder if Southampton have got anything more on that job? It's their pigeon really.'

The lorry had actually been hi-jacked in the Southampton police area. They had notified the Yard at once, realising that the cameras which had been stolen could only be disposed of in London, and the case had been passed on to Heaton. There just might be a link with this murder, or there might not.

Field didn't answer.

After a moment Heaton said: 'I'm not happy about this man Rawson.'

'Why not?'

'I don't quite know.'

He frowned. Often in the past he had been 'not too happy' about witnesses, and, frequently, what he had taken for guilt had only been nervousness, which had worsened as his suspicions had increased, creating a kind of vicious circle. He was now reluctant to assume anyone guilty merely because of the way he felt about them, yet he wasn't sure that Rawson's manner had been entirely due to nervousness.

'He found the body,' he went on, 'and he seems honest enough, yet all the time I was talking to him I had the feeling that he was holding something back. There's another coincidence, too. Both Rawson and the dead man are photographers.'

'That's not unreasonable,' Field put in. 'One calling on the other and finding him dead.'

He waited while Heaton pulled at his lip.

'That doesn't work,' the Superintendent said at last. 'They weren't friendly. Far from it, according to what Rawson's already told me.'

'Professional jealousy?' Field hazarded.

Heaton shrugged. 'Could be. Hardly seems strong enough for murder, though, and the fact that this girl was being followed has got to fit in somewhere.'

Field shrugged as Heaton pulled the phone towards him, intending to call Jean Dixon and tell her he was coming round to see her. As he dialled, Field said:

'Talking of Records, I have the impression that the name Dixon has been connected with a photographer recently.'

Before Heaton could make any comment his phone shrilled briefly and a voice said: 'Your Chelsea call.'

Another man's voice came on, questioning, a faint note of anger in it. 'Hello?'

'Could I speak to Miss Dixon, please?'

'Jean?'

'That's right.'

There was a faint sound as the phone at the other end was banged down on to a table, then the noise of footsteps walking away. Heaton waited, wondering why the man had said 'Jean' in a tone of voice which implied that there was more than one Miss Dixon. He wondered if Rawson knew that, and if he did, why he hadn't mentioned it the night before.

A girl's voice said: 'Hello?'

'Good morning, Miss Dixon. I'm Chief Superintendent Heaton from Scotland Yard. I'd like to come round and see you, if I may?'

'What about?' The girl was suddenly cautious, and a little breathless.

'Nothing to worry about, Miss Dixon. Just a few routine questions. I'll come round in half an hour, if that's convenient to you.' He waited until she had agreed that it was, then rang off before she had time to say anything more.

'Never tell them why you're coming if they don't already know,' he said to Field without looking up, although at the back of his mind he knew that Jean would realise what he was after as soon as she read those few lines in the morning papers. There was no answer from Field, and he looked up, to see him speaking on the other phone. When he had finished, he gave him an enquiring glance.

'I've just been on to Records,' Field answered. 'They don't know anything at all about a Jean Dixon, so I took a chance and got on to Photography. They don't know anything about her, either, but — ' He paused slightly, and then went on: ' — they have heard of another girl, a model called Sonia Dixon. I don't know if there's any connection between the two of them, but it does look a bit suspicious, doesn't it?'

A model. Two photographers.

Heaton said: 'It's a start. I wonder why Rawson never mentioned her last night? After all, it's part of his job to know these characters, and, if he knows Jean, he should know her sister. I had an idea that he was lying last night.'

He paused, then went on grimly: 'If he

was, I'll have it out of the girl in half an hour. While I'm there I'll have a word with Sonia, too.'

★ ★ ★

Thirty-five minutes later, Heaton stood in the flat thinking over what Jean Dixon had just told him about her sister's disappearance, and about the policeman who had called last night. He wondered what the Division had wanted with her; fortunately, it would be fairly easy to find that out.

The girl was watching him anxiously, the man, as if he didn't care.

Could Sonia have had anything to do with Roxy's death? He frowned, and the troubled look in Jean Dixon's eyes intensified.

There was a ring at the door.

He saw Rawson come into the room.

He said: 'Good morning, Mr. Rawson, I'm glad you've called round. There are one or two things here that don't quite fit in with what you've told me.'

Rawson came in slowly, nodding to

Cartney, smiling at Jean. Once he realised just how much Heaton knew, he guessed that Cartney had done his best to implicate Sonia.

Heaton asked: 'Could Sonia have gone away before the murder was committed, so that later it would look as though she had had nothing to do with it?'

'I don't think that she's vanished,' Rawson answered. 'I think that she's been kidnapped for some reason. You don't understand what this Wesloe contract means to her, and the jobs that always come to the girl who models Wesloe's new range of exclusives. It would have been the last stage of her career.'

'But suppose she wanted Roxy dead more than she valued her career?'

'I can't think of any reason why she should want him dead,' Rawson told him. 'She disliked him, but that isn't the same thing. In any case, you don't know what these models are like. They're only interested in their looks and their careers. Personally, I think that Roxy kidnapped her, and that if she killed him at all, it was in self-defence.'

'Unfortunately, Mr. Rawson, I can't work on what you think personally, I have to work on facts. For instance, you say you think that Roxy kidnapped her?'

Heaton nodded, a little ponderously.

'That's right.'

'What grounds have you for saying that?'

Rawson hesitated. Cartney was watching him, a faintly puzzled look on his face, Jean was sitting very still on the settee, her hand on the back of the poodle's head, her eyes very bright.

He said slowly: 'I can't give you a definite reason. If I could, then perhaps none of this would ever have arisen.' He stopped. This was dangerous ground. Say too much and it could make Sonia the obvious suspect — if she could be any more obvious than she was now.

'Go on,' Heaton urged him.

'What else can I say?' Rawson demanded. 'I know as much as you do, probably less. I can't give you any more help.'

Heaton, still standing, looked at him,

his head on one side. 'Are you sure?' he asked. 'You sounded so confident before. Are you sure that you're holding nothing back?'

10

Heaton Probes

Rawson said briefly: 'Why should I be holding anything back?'

There was a pause. Although he could know nothing of what Rawson had found by Roxy's body, there was still something disconcerting about the look in Heaton's eyes. There was always a chance, too, that he had found out something other than the shoe, something which would condemn Sonia even more.

Eventually, Heaton said: 'You were the first person there, Mr. Rawson. I must be certain that you left everything exactly as it was when you got there.'

Rawson's hands clenched. Why did Heaton have to keep hammering this point? He said: 'Superintendent, you keep asking me that. Is there any reason why I should have disturbed anything?'

Heaton spoke easily. 'No real reason,

Mr. Rawson. It's just that the discovery must have come as a great shock to you, whatever you thought of Roxy personally. In those circumstances it would be a moment or two before you knew properly what you were doing, and in that time you might have moved something. People do, you know.'

His voice now was very mild, as if he realised that he had been driving Rawson too hard.

'There have been cases where witnesses have moved things which seemed unimportant to them but which turned out later to be vital. It makes it very difficult for the police when something like that happens.'

Rawson thought that he was justified in shouting now, that he could do it without attracting further attention to himself.

'For the last time,' he cried, 'I've done nothing that I haven't told you about. Now, either stop persecuting me or get out.'

As soon as he had said it, he regretted the last sentence. From the corner of his eye he saw Cartney stir, as if he were about to make some angry comment, but he said nothing.

Heaton drew a deep breath. 'I don't think that you can help me much further, Mr. Rawson. If there is anything, perhaps you'll get in touch with me.' He went to the door, and opened it. 'Good morning.' He smiled at Jean and Cartney. 'Thank you for being so helpful.'

The door closed.

Cartney said: 'All right, Rawson. Now tell us what you were hiding from him.'

From the settee Jean said: 'Mike, you're as bad as that policeman.'

'No I'm not.' Cartney got out of his chair and went over to where Rawson was sitting. 'He was holding something back, that's definite. Weren't you?' By now he was very near to Rawson, leaning over him, gripping the arms of his chair so tightly that his fingers turned white with the pressure.

'I — '

'Don't try and give me any nonsense,' Cartney said harshly. 'You were too emphatic with him for that. What do you know that you haven't told him?'

Rawson looked at him. He could tell him about the shoe, of course, but that wasn't the main problem. More worrying was the thought that if Cartney had found him so obvious what had Heaton deduced? Was that why he had been pushing the questions? Had he been hoping to produce some effect like this while he was still here?

Above him, Cartney was leering down. When he made no answer one of his hands moved from the arm of the chair and gripped Rawson's collar.

Jean shouted: 'Mike — '

Cartney released Rawson and turned to her. 'You keep out of this for a minute. I'm going to find out what he knows if I have to break his neck to do it.'

He turned back to Rawson.

'Well?' he demanded. 'What is it? Have you got proof that Sonia was definitely there last night when Roxy was killed? Is that what you're trying to hide?'

He leered.

That was the moment when Rawson remembered that Cartney had a key to this flat, and that nothing would have been easier than for him to come here while Jean was out, and get one of Sonia's shoes.

At that moment, the doorbell rang.

The tension in the room was eased by the sudden shrilling of sound. Jean stood up and crossed to the door. As she went into the hall, Cartney spoke again.

'Another thing, Rawson, is that you don't order people out of this flat. Either I do, or Jean does. You don't.'

'Listen, Cartney,' Rawson said suddenly, 'don't you think you're making a bit too much out of all this? After all, we both want the same thing. You want to keep Jean safe, I want to do the same for Sonia. If she didn't kill Roxy, I want to know who did.'

'What do you mean, if she didn't kill him?'

Cartney broke off abruptly. A bright flash of light came from near the front door. Jean staggered back into the room and screamed.

Cartney crossed the room with one stride, Rawson close behind him. Jean was standing by the hall door, very still. Near her was a man, who was making no attempt to get away or to do anything. While Cartney put his arm round Jean's shoulders Rawson went past him to the man at the door.

'What the hell do you want?' he demanded.

'I'm sorry.' It was a second man, standing behind the first one, who spoke. 'It was my fault. I suppose I shouldn't have done it that way.'

He came farther into the room, and Rawson saw that he was carrying a camera with a powerful flash unit attached to it. The first man spoke, in a strong Scottish accent.

'We're from the *Echo*. We thought you might give us a story. When the young lady opened the door, my colleague here took a picture. I think that the flash took her by surprise.'

Rawson was reminded of the way he

had surprised Sonia two days ago. Somehow, it seemed weeks ago.

Cartney was still holding Jean. 'I ought to break both your necks,' he said. 'She's already upset. You don't know what you could have done to her.'

'I'm all right, Mike.' Jean's voice was faint, but firm. 'It just took me my surprise, that was all.'

The men were making no attempt to go away.

'Which of you is Mr. Rawson?' the Scot demanded.

'I am. Why?' Rawson said.

'Thank you, sir. You found the body, I believe?'

'I did.' There was no harm in telling them this; it had been in the earlier reports.

'Why did you go to see the dead man?'

'I felt like it,' Rawson answered. 'Look, you've been told once. Get out.' He glanced across at Cartney, not surprised to find him too preoccupied with Jean to notice much of what was going on.

'Just a few words,' the Scot urged.

'Can't you see that we aren't in any mood to answer your questions? The last thing we want at the moment is a bunch of newspaper men here.'

'One of the things you've got to accept if you find a murdered man. Most people don't mind, they like to see their names in the papers. Do your business a lot of good, too,' he added.

'I shouldn't think so,' Rawson said. 'My clients aren't the type who're attracted by things like that. They'd be more likely to find another photographer.'

The Scot was irrepressible. 'Where's the missing model?' he asked. 'How does she fit in with this?'

Rawson hesitated. There had naturally been nothing about Sonia in the morning papers, so that meant that Heaton must have told them very recently. Now they knew about her there would be no keeping them away. She would be the sex interest in the case; they would have plenty of pictures of her in the files which they could use to catch the reader's attention.

He said: 'She's got nothing to do with it.'

'Hasn't she? Why's she gone away, then, especially with this contract you've got?'

Cartney came across from Jean. 'Get out,' he said shortly.

'Is that Sonia's sister? I wonder if we could just have another picture?' The photographer moved round.

Cartney looked at Rawson. 'How much is this camera worth?'

'A couple of hundred pounds.'

'Will it be insured?'

'I imagine so.'

'Then if I smash it up it'll be all right.' Cartney caught hold of the photographer's shoulder and pulled him round. The man's hands were encumbered by the heavy camera; he could put up no resistance as he was hustled to the door and pushed into the corridor.

'Your turn next,' Cartney said to the Scot.

'All right, I'm going.' He turned and followed his colleague out.

Cartney slammed the door.

'How did they know about Sonia?' he demanded. 'Did you tell them?'

'Why should I tell them? I was hoping to keep it from the police, so I certainly wouldn't tell the Press.'

'Then Heaton must have passed it on when he found out. I've a good mind to tell him what I think of him.'

He crossed to the phone and picked up the receiver, dialling quickly.

Jean called: 'Mike, be careful what you say.'

'Superintendent Heaton, please.' There was a pause, then they heard Cartney putting his complaint in a low, grim voice. Suddenly, he stopped speaking, and listened for what seemed a long time. Rawson waited for an angry outburst, but it never came; eventually Cartney said: 'Thank you,' and hung up.

He turned to face them.

'No one at the Yard has mentioned Sonia or the fact that she's missing,' he stated flatly.

Rawson's eyes narrowed, and Cartney remained by the phone, one hand on top of it.

It was Jean who said what they were all thinking. 'Then, in that case, how could those men know that she is missing?'

'Unless,' Rawson said, 'they know where she is.'

11

Threat to the Contract

There was nothing else they could do. The natural assumption had been that the men were not reporters at all, but had come round to see what the police were doing, and what Rawson and the others had thought. A simple phone call to the *Echo* had disproved this. Two men had been sent round, they were told, one of them a Scot. The initial information had come in the form of an anonymous phone call.

'You can't blame us for following it up,' the Editor had said. 'The case of the missing model. It's just the thing to catch the public's attention. You can't blame us.'

Rawson thanked him and hung up, then they sat in silence, considering the implications of the phone call. Rawson had the fact that Cartney could easily have got hold of one of Sonia's shoes to consider, too. If he knew that the shoe was there, and he had left it there deliberately to incriminate Sonia, that would explain his insistence that Rawson was holding something back from the police, and his determination to find out. He wondered if she had more than one pair of shoes with the 'S' on the front, or if she had come home to change them after leaving his studio. Sometime later, when Cartney wasn't there, he intended to see Jean and ask her about this. It would be interesting, too, to see if the other shoe was there.

There was only one thing wrong with all this.

Cartney had no motive for killing Roxy and trying to put it on Sonia.

The phone began to ring loudly.

The silence in the room was broken as Jean stood up and snatched up the receiver. She listened for what seemed a long time, then said:

'Yes, I'm afraid it is true.'

She spoke so softly that Rawson only just caught the words. He glanced away from where Cartney was sitting staring at him; the words could only refer to Sonia.

Jean was saying: 'As a matter of fact, he's here now if you want to speak to him.'

Cartney glanced across at her, but she offered the phone to Rawson.

She said: 'Wesloe's.'

Wesloe's.

The dress people for whom they were doing the photos. They had insisted on having Sonia, even though he had suggested to her that it was his own idea, and Jacob Wesloe had told him that without her the photos would be useless. They intended to feature her in all their advertising, to make her in effect Miss Wesloe, and only her face would do for them.

They couldn't have Sonia now.

The contract was important to all of them. To Wesloe's because of the increased business they hoped for, to Sonia because of the opportunity it represented, and to Rawson because if he did it well the word would soon get round and he would find himself in great

112

demand. If he failed he would finish like Roxy, on the verge of bankruptcy, scratching around for work.

He was conscious of all this as he took the phone, yet one thought stood out above all the others.

Had Wesloe's had an anonymous phone call, too?

He spoke into the receiver. 'Rawson.'

Jacob Wesloe himself answered. 'They tell me that Sonia Dixon has vanished and that she's suspected of murder.'

'She's vanished. How did you know?'

'I had a phone call. Anonymous, but in a matter like this I have to do something. You do understand, don't you?' He seemed almost apologetic. 'These are important pictures, Mr. Rawson, and I must have Sonia in them. On the other hand, I need them quickly, and to have a suspected murderess associated with our name isn't going to help us much, either.'

Rawson didn't answer.

Wesloe said: 'Mr. Rawson, unless Sonia is back tomorrow and you can show me uncontestable proof that she has nothing to do with this murder, I shall have to

113

cancel the contract.'

For a moment Rawson didn't answer. When he did he said: 'Mr. Wesloe, can I come round and see you?'

★ ★ ★

Wesloe's factory and offices were situated in the East End of London, a new factory on a former bombed site with the offices in an adjoining building that had stood there throughout the war. The building was set back from the pavement, and there was enough space in front of it to park two cars without interfering with pedestrians. Both spaces were taken now; one by a Rover which he knew belonged to Jacob Wesloe, and the other by an older sports car.

He drove into the yard and was stopped by a man in overalls.

'You can't come in here. It's private ground.'

Rawson felt in his pocket, took out one of his cards and handed it to the man, saying that he had an appointment with Wesloe. The man read the card, looked

114

doubtful for a moment, then pointed to the far side of the yard.

'You can put it over there,' he said, 'but leave room for the van to get out.'

Rawson moved off, parked his car and returned to the office. To reach the main entrance he had to go out of the yard again, on to the pavement, and through glass swing doors to a small window with 'Please knock' painted on it in small neatly formed letters.

He knocked.

An elderly woman opened it; Rawson could see the magazine on her knees as she tried to slide it beneath the switchboard in front of her. He asked for Mr. Wesloe, gave his name and watched as she plugged a cord into the board, pulled a switch, spoke quickly then let the switch flick back, the cord pop into its hole.

'I think you know the way, don't you?'

Rawson nodded and went through the door that led off the room. For a moment he heard the sound of sewing machines, deafening to someone unused to it, then he was at Wesloe's door. This opened off a quieter part of the factory, but Rawson knew that the room was soundproofed. The two buildings, the old and the new, had been run together very cleverly so that there was hardly any walking from one to the other, and the new one supported the old.

He tapped at Wesloe's door.

He heard Wesloe call to him and went in, letting the door shut behind him.

Wesloe stepped out from behind a desk littered with papers and folders. On one of the piles of loose sheets was a head, about the size of an orange, carved from black wood. It had been a present from one of Wesloe's overseas customers and was now used as a paperweight. Also on the desk were a number of large sheets of paper, obviously patterns for some kind of coat.

The desk filled most of the room. The rest of the space was taken up by two green filing cabinets and a large gas fire which was switched on full. It made the room far too hot; on a cold day it would be pleasant to come into, but now it would soon become unbearable.

Wesloe shook hands, then turned back to the desk, clearing away the patterns.

'Another problem,' he said as he put them on the floor. 'A new designer of mine, not long out of school, has made half these to the wrong size. It wasn't discovered until we'd cut up most of the cloth involved.' He shook his head. 'She should never have been allowed to do them on her own.'

His tone became brisker.

'Still, you've problems of your own, haven't you, Mr. Rawson? Let's hear what you can tell me about Sonia.'

He indicated a chair, and Rawson sat down slowly.

'Has it occurred to you, Mr. Wesloe,' he said, 'that you might be the cause of her disappearance?'

12

Responsibility

For a few moments, Wesloe showed no reaction to this statement. He played with a corner of his blotter, green blotting paper held by large black triangles, then he reached out and moved the carved head a little to one side. Behind him, the gas fire hissed.

He said: 'Explain what you mean, Mr. Rawson. How can I possibly be responsible?'

'Very easily.' Rawson settled himself back in his chair; to put this over properly he would have to be relaxed and confident. 'The designs which we've already photographed, and the ones which we were going to do in the future were your new designs for an exclusive summer range. Right?'

'Correct,' Wesloe said formally.

'As I see it, the designs themselves

wouldn't be worth very much if they were offered for sale. In other words, there wouldn't be much chance of stealing them and selling at a profit.'

Wesloe nodded.

'On the other hand,' Rawson went on, 'suppose they were stolen, copied and mass produced.'

'You can't do that,' Wesloe objected. 'Either a design is suitable for quantity production or it isn't. None of these are. They're designed expressly for a limited run of hand-made garments.'

'Possibly they are, but suppose the object wasn't to mass produce them at a profit, but merely to mass produce them. To flood the market with copies of dresses that influential women have paid a high price for. What would be the result then?'

'In terms of damage to Wesloe's?'

Rawson nodded.

'It would be immense. We'd lose half our clientele overnight. I still say that it couldn't happen, though. Once we knew that the designs had been stolen we wouldn't make them. We'd have to start all over again.'

'Exactly,' Rawson agreed. 'Could you still catch the summer market?'

Wesloe hesitated. 'Well, no,' he admitted finally. 'We'd lose this summer's trade.'

'Plus the money you've spent so far?'

'That would be a lot, naturally, but hardly enough to break us, Mr. Rawson. We aren't a tiny back-street firm who can be intimidated by a threat like that. I can't see it as a feasible proposition, I'm afraid.'

Rawson was silent, trying to think of some other point that might be more convincing to Wesloe.

Wesloe went on: 'Besides, what would be the point of doing anything like that?'

'Do you know of anyone with a grudge against the firm? Anyone you've sacked recently or anything like that?'

Wesloe shook his head, looking almost smug.

'You won't find your reason there, Mr. Rawson. We have extremely good relations with the staff here, so good that not only have we not dismissed anyone for a number of years, but we're one of the few factories in this business where the unions can get no kind of a foothold, however hard they try.'

Rawson seized on this.

'Are you sure that the unions aren't behind this?'

Wesloe laughed out loud.

'You're talking of a respectable union now,' he said, 'not a bunch of crooks. I know they may appear like that sometimes, but they aren't really. The only reason they haven't been able to get in here is not because we don't want them at our throats in the boardroom, but because the workers can see no advantage in belonging to a union. They aren't going to pay for something that isn't any use to them, are they?'

'Perhaps not,' Rawson was forced to admit. 'I still say that there must be some connection between this and the contract. Nothing like this has ever happened before; I've never had a contract like this before. The two must be connected.'

'Has Sonia ever argued with Roxy before?' Wesloe enquired mildly.

'How did you know that?'

'Things get around. I have more models than Sonia working for me, you know, and some of them also work for Roxy. I knew some time ago that she didn't like working for him. That was partly why I rejected his tender.'

'Did Roxy know that?'

'Not so far as I'm aware. The reason for that decision should never have gone beyond myself and the other directors.'

'But could he have found it out in some way?' Rawson persisted.

Wesloe shrugged. 'The typist who did the minutes could have passed it on, I suppose, although that's very doubtful. She's been with the firm for nearly thirty years, and she's not the type who goes about blabbing confidential information.' He paused. 'I can see your point, of course. You think that Roxy was trying to get some kind of revenge, she found out and in the ensuing argument she killed him.'

'Something like that could have happened,' Rawson agreed. 'There's one thing that doesn't really fit in with anything.'

'What's that?'

'You had an anonymous phone call,' Rawson said slowly. 'The *Echo* had one, too. Both of them stressed that Sonia was missing, and both of them had the result that some kind of pressure was put on me. I think that's significant, but I can't see how.'

'Do the police know of these calls?'

'They know of the first one to the *Echo*.'

'I see.' Wesloe took up the blotter again. 'And what have they to say?'

'There isn't very much they can say. At the time they were told there had only been one call. That wasn't sufficient to base a theory on.'

'Then don't you think that you'd be better to tell them about the second call?' Wesloe asked, pushing the phone towards Rawson.

'I'd rather go round and see them about it than ring them,' he answered.

'Why is that?'

Rawson grinned. 'Because I'm regarded as hiding information from them, for some reason. If I go round and tell them this, it might go a long way towards getting me off the hook and letting them concentrate on the real villains.'

'I see.' Wesloe was still toying with his blotter.

Rawson watched him. So far there had been nothing encouraging in the conversation, and, privately, he agreed with all Wesloe had said. As a motive, his theory was fantastic, and could produce very little profit for anybody, even someone with a grudge against the firm. However, there was the contract to think of, and any method of saving that had to be used to full effect. He was trying to think of another way of presenting his argument when Wesloe said:

'In view of what you've told me, Mr. Rawson, I'm prepared to keep an open mind on the subject. You go and see the police about these phone calls, see what they say and keep me informed. Don't worry about the contract for the moment. We can afford to wait a week or so.'

He signed for Rawson to leave.

★ ★ ★

Rawson drove slowly out of Wesloe's yard. There were several things he could do now. He could go to the police, as he had told Wesloe he intended to do; he could go back to the studio and ring the police later; he could go to Jean's; or he could go to Roxy's.

If he went to the police, he would be liable to find himself facing more questioning from Heaton, possibly much harsher than it had been before. He knew that he could keep his denial up for some time yet, but he felt that in the face of continued and expert questioning he would be sure to let something slip, and give away the fact that the shoe had been there.

Should he have told Heaton about that and implicated Sonia from the start? Would the police have assumed that because her shoe was there and she had now vanished she had killed Roxy? What was it that Heaton had said; he had to deal in facts. These were facts; they proved that Sonia had been there and that she might have something to hide. That something, Heaton would have to assume, was the fact that she had killed Roxy.

Could he convince them otherwise? Not on the facts so far available, and until he could it would be a battle between him and the police; he had to find the real killer before the police found Sonia.

If he went back to Jean's, all he was likely to find was another argument with Cartney.

Cartney puzzled him. He had the chance to get some of Sonia's shoes, he had apparently pressed the point in an attempt to make Rawson admit that one had been by the body, but yet he had no motive at all and, as Jean's fiancé, he was a most unlikely suspect.

That only left the choice of going back to his own studio or to Roxy's. There would be nothing at his own place; he decided to go to Roxy's. He swung the car off to the right and began to move quickly through the traffic. At length he turned the corner into Shaftesbury Avenue, cutting sharply between a bus and a taxi. Behind him a horn sounded loudly; he reflected that he would have to be more careful or there would be no one to help Sonia, then came to the small street where Roxy's studio was.

The studio that had been Roxy's.

He stopped the car where he had left it the previous evening.

The shop door was open. He pushed it cautiously, thinking that the police might be there, then pushed it harder. Even if they were, it was too late to draw back now, and in any event, as a photographer himself, he had a flimsy excuse for going there.

Everything was very much as it had been the night before except that the cover had been taken off the typewriter and there was a sheet of paper in the carriage, and a girl's coat, green with a fur collar, hung on a peg behind the desk.

There was no one in the receptionist's chair.

For an instant he thought that the place had been closed for the day and the staff sent home, but the coat seemed to disprove that.

He hesitated, then crossed to the stairs. The door that led to them was closed, but not locked. He turned the handle and peered up into the gloom. There was nothing to suggest that anyone was up there, but there was nowhere else they could be, and he started to climb them, keeping the sound of his footsteps low. Memories of the previous night came back to him vividly as he did so, and he paused, peering into the shadows, half fancying that he saw someone lurking there.

Still there was no sound.

He moved up another stair and stopped again.

From somewhere, he seemed to hear a faint noise. Wishing that he knew where the light switch was he climbed to the top and stood uncertainly.

Suddenly, a man's voice came clearly, harshly.

'Well? Where is he?'

It was followed by a sob, and then a shrill scream.

13

Scream

Silence fell after the scream, while Rawson hesitated on the stairs. Suddenly, he turned and hurried down them as silently as he had climbed. If he caught the man and overpowered him there was always a chance that he might try to run, much as Bradford had done the night before, and with the street door locked there was a greater chance of catching up with him again. After slipping the catch on the door, he hurried back to the top of the stairs, in time to hear a voice say:

'You know where he is! Don't come the little innocent with us.'

He? Us?

How many men were there?

And were they the men who had been in the van which had nearly knocked him down? If they were, then they had had no scruples about trying to kill him then, and presumably would have none now.

The voices settled to a low murmuring, of which he could distinguish no words. Padding softly down the corridor, he passed three doors, all shut, and from behind any one of which the voices could have come. He wished that someone would speak loudly again so that he could be certain which one it was, but even the murmuring seemed to have died away now. He paused at one of the doors and pressed his ear to it; there was only silence on the other side. The remaining two were the same, but from behind one right at the end, the room where he had found the body, came the soft murmering, the words more distant now.

One of the voices was a girl's. She was saying:

'Why should I know where he is? He doesn't tell me everything. I don't know anything about it!'

Her voice rose at the end of the sentence, until it was almost a squeak.

A man's voice, different from the one which had spoken before, answered:

'We'll have to make you tell us.'

The girl cried out: 'How can you make me if I don't know?'

Rawson tried the door, expecting it to be locked. To his surprise, it opened easily. Three people were in the room, two men and the girl. The men had their backs to him, but the girl, bound to a chair, was in the middle of the room, facing him. She wore a neat blue skirt and white jumper, but the jumper had been pushed up over her breasts, so that her stomach was bare. One of the men had a cigarette in his mouth; he drew on it hard until the tip glowed red, then took it from his lips and looked at it.

He grinned as he moved towards the girl. Her eyes widened in fear, and the flesh quivered then contracted sharply as the glowing tip came very close.

Rawson said: 'Stop that!'

The man whirled round, the cigarette falling from his fingers.

'Who the hell are you?'

He moved closer, watching the two men. 'That doesn't matter.'

One of the men was moving away from the other; at the moment he could see

131

both at once, but that would shortly be impossible.

'Keep still!'

'What if I don't?'

Both the men were young, about Bradford's age. One of them was much shorter than Rawson, with a faint wisp of a moustache; the other, the one who had the cigarette, was not only taller, but heavier built. Rawson gave him most of his attention, giving no answer to the other's question, just waiting warily.

The attack wasn't long in coming.

Both men rushed together, as if they had practised the manoeuvre and knew exactly what to do. Ignoring the smaller man, Rawson kicked out at the other. It was a lucky blow, catching the big man on his shin and sending him back against the wall. His head hit the plaster; he staggered and fell. The small man was still running in, his arms working. If any of the blows had landed anywhere important they would have been crippling, but because of his greater height, Rawson was able to keep out of range.

The big man was on his knees.

Rawson moved towards him, the smaller man followed. Suddenly Rawson stopped. The man rushed at him, his arms still working. He caught one of them, pulled the man off balance and threw him over his leg against the wall. He hit it with the top of his head and fell, obviously unconscious.

The girl sat very still.

The big man rushed, not at Rawson, but round him.

Rawson tried to catch him, missed his footing and staggered. The man reached the door, wrenched it open and ran down the passage, his feet pounding. Rawson started after him, then stopped. With the small man here, there was no need to catch the other.

Rawson crossed back to the girl, took out his knife and cut the ropes which bound her. She sat still when he had done so then began to rub her wrists where the cords had made red marks.

She said: 'They were going to burn me.'

'It's all over now. They won't hurt you again.'

She nodded, and pulled the jumper down. A handkerchief was still tucked incongruously in one of the sleeves; she took it out and blew her nose hard.

She said: 'Who are you?'

Her voice was still shrill with the terror she must have felt before.

'Never mind that for the moment. Let me deal with this character first.'

The man was coming round now, groaning slightly as he lay slumped against the wall. Carefully, Rawson bent down and pulled his arm; when he let it go the man fell back limply. He turned to the girl.

'Who were they after?'

She opened her mouth to speak, then suddenly cried: 'Look out!'

Rawson whirled. The man was on his feet preparing to spring at him. As he moved, Rawson ducked, and the man somersaulted over him, carried on by his own fury. Rawson felt the pain in his neck as the man went over, then there was a cry from behind him. He stood up, a little dazed, thankful that it hadn't been the big man who had done that.

'Get up.'

The man on the floor sneered at him. Even when he was lying still the energy in him seemed to be visible; everything about him, even his words, was packed with a savage fury.

'Get up.' Rawson stepped nearer.

The man got to his knees, and he stood over him.

'Stay like that. You're safer that way.'

'You're afraid,' the man sneered.

'Not afraid,' Rawson said quietly. 'Just sensible. Now, tell me what you want.'

The man spat upwards at him.

Rawson picked him up by his collar. The short arms worked helplessly as he hung, a dead weight, swaying slightly, then he dropped as Rawson let go.

'Tell me what you want.'

'I want to know where Norden is.'

'Why?'

'That should be obvious.' The man gasped slightly.

'Not to me it isn't. You'll have to explain it.'

'I'm explaining nothing. What do you think Harry'd do if I told you everything?'

'Who's Harry? And who's Norden, come to that?'

The man moved slightly, still kneeling. Rawson made as if to pick him up again, and he cowered away, a thin trickle of saliva running down his chin.

'Oh, God,' he said. 'If I don't split, you get me. If I do, Harry gets me. What the hell can I do?'

Rawson grinned faintly. 'I'm here now, Harry isn't,' he said. 'I should split. Start by telling me who Harry is.'

'If you don't know him what's the use in telling you?'

Rawson reached out again.

'Wait!' the man cried, saliva bubbling at his lips. 'His name's Harry Spencer. I don't know any more than that.'

'And who are you?'

'Do you have to know that? What about the other bloke who was here? His name is — '

He broke off abruptly, hurled himself upwards and butted Rawson's stomach with his head.

He ran for the door.

By the time Rawson had recovered

from the blow, the man was well away from the studio.

★ ★ ★

The girl sat on the chair behind the desk. After the two men had gone the fear in her eyes had shown no signs of dying away; if anything, it was worse than it had been. She had told Rawson that she had come to work as usual that morning, knowing nothing of the murder, and that the police, who had been there when she arrived, had told her what had happened. They had only stayed for a short while afterwards, leaving her in charge, and telling her to contact them at once if anything further happened.

The two men had come about ten minutes before Rawson. They had dragged her up the stairs, tied her to the chair and started to question her; when she wouldn't tell them what they wanted to know they had threatened to burn her with a cigarette until she did.

When she had finished Rawson asked: 'And who's this Norden that they're so anxious about? Do you know where he is?'

She leaned forward suddenly, pushing the typewriter out of the way, the fear replaced by something else. She gripped his arm painfully over the desk, and burst out:

'He's my boyfriend. He — he's vanished and I'm sure that if I tell the police they'll think that he's killed Mr. Roxy!'

14

Dick Norden

The girl was very near to tears. Rawson hesitated fractionally then moved round the desk.

'Why should they think that?'

'Because he isn't here this morning.'

'Perhaps there's some good reason for that,' Rawson suggested. 'He might be ill or something.'

The girl took her arm away from his, reached for the handkerchief in her sleeve again and blew her nose. She screwed up the handkerchief and pushed it back, making a bulge in the wool.

'He wasn't ill yesterday.'

'Who's been here from the police?' Rawson asked.

'I didn't find out his name.'

'Superintendent Heaton? Smallish chap?'

'He wore a uniform.'

That cleared up one thing at least; the

question of how Heaton could have been there before going to Jean's. Heaton didn't wear a uniform; that meant that he hadn't been here yet this morning, but might come at any time.

'Have you told the police he's missing?'

'Not yet,' the girl replied. 'When they left, he was only twenty minutes late and there was nothing to suggest that he wasn't going to come in.'

'Have you tried to get in touch with him?'

'Of course I've tried!' Her voice was sharp. 'He's on the phone at home, but I can't get an answer.' She paused as if deciding whether or not to trust him. 'He lives with a relation, an aunt, I think,' she said impulsively. 'She doesn't go to work, and even if Dick isn't in she should be answering the phone. I don't know where he is. He — he's always told me before when he hasn't been coming to work.'

She stopped speaking and stared at him. To gain a little time to think, Rawson asked her her name.

She shrugged. 'No harm in telling you that. I'm Pam Woods.'

'Is there harm in telling me anything?'

'There could be. You could be like the police and those men and be after Dick.'

Rawson spoke very gently, leaning over the desk. 'Why should I want to find Dick? I'm not the police; I'm not even a private detective. I'm just another photographer.'

'That's what you say.' Pam picked up the card that he had given her earlier on. 'After all, anyone could have had this printed.'

'Ring the number if you want. They'll soon tell you whether or not I'm genuine.'

Pam said: 'Even if I did there could be someone there who's been told to say that you're a photographer. That wouldn't help at all.' She ran her hand across her forehead, brushing away a strand of hair that had strayed from the bun into which her hair was drawn. 'Why don't you just give up and go back to Scotland Yard, or wherever you've come from?'

Rawson hesitated, wondering what he could say to convince her.

She went on: 'If you are just a photographer, why have you come here?

I've never seen you before and you weren't a friend of Mr. Roxy's.' She half stood up, her voice squeaking slightly. 'Why have you come here?'

Rawson spoke softly, almost whispering, so that the girl had to lean closer in order to hear him.

'Have you told the police anything about either Dick or his aunt?'

'No.'

Rawson spoke carefully; the wrong word here could completely destroy his chances.

'Suppose I go round to Norden's, just to make sure nothing's wrong?'

Pam considered, then reached under the desk, pulled out the phone book, flipped to the page with Rawson's name on it, and pushed it back, after comparing the number there with the one on his card.

'All right,' she said simply. 'I don't see what harm you can do. Will you phone me or something after you've been?'

He nodded and she gave him the address. As he turned to leave, he remembered something.

'Any idea who Harry Spencer is?'

'He used to come here sometimes, to see Mr. Roxy. I never liked him. He used to look at you and chuckle, but it wasn't a normal chuckle. There was something horrible in the way he did it.'

'Any idea where he lives?'

She shuddered. 'I never bothered to find out. I didn't want him to think I was interested in him, did I?' She stood up and began to look through a card index. 'It may be in here.' After a moment she shook her head and banged the drawer shut, 'It isn't there.'

'Perhaps Norden will know. Is he one of Spencer's friends, too?'

'That's something else I can't understand,' Pam said. 'Spencer never used to bother with him before. Why should he suddenly be so anxious to find him?'

'We'll know better about that once we know why he's gone,' Rawson answered. 'I'll call you later.'

When he got outside, a policeman was walking slowly towards the car, apparently taking no notice of it. Rawson got in, started the engine and drove off slowly; the policeman's head moved slightly, and he nodded as the car passed him.

The mid-morning traffic was quite heavy now. Above, the sun was trying to break through heavily banked cloud; from time to time a ray of light glinted on the bonnet. He inched his way along Shaftesbury Avenue, then headed south towards Clapham, where Norden lived with his aunt in a bungalow, one of a row of six, set well back from the road.

He stopped his car some distance away, trying to decide what was the best method of approach. The bungalows were normal suburban types, small gardens back and front, neat gates and drives. Eventually, he drove on slowly and stopped outside number thirty-four. Seen close to, it was obvious that it had just been repainted. Even on this dull day, the woodwork was bright and clean; blue window frames and guttering, the sills of the windows white.

Before he had time to change his mind about what he was going to do he left the car, went up the path to the house, and rang the bell. When the door opened he saw a large, bony woman glaring at him. Her hair was drawn tightly back, emphasising her prominent cheekbones, and she wore a flowered apron over a woollen jumper and skirt.

'Well?' she demanded.

'I'm looking for Dick Norden,' Rawson said pleasantly. 'I believe he lives here.'

'Why do you want him?'

'I work with him. He hasn't turned up this morning, and when I phoned earlier I couldn't get an answer. I thought I'd come round, seeing that I was in this area anyway, and see if there was anything wrong.'

The woman's expression softened very slightly. 'I must have been out when you rang,' she said. 'I don't know about not turning up for work. He wasn't here last night; he went to stay with one of his aunts in Watford. You'll have to ask her where he is. Just a minute and I'll get you the address.'

She turned and went back into the bungalow, leaving the door partly open. She wasn't gone for long, but long enough for Rawson to make sure that what he had thought he had seen before was, in fact, there. When the woman returned, she handed him a piece of paper with a Watford address and phone number on it.

'I'm sure you'll find everything all right,' she said. 'He's not the boy to stay off work without a good reason, isn't Dick.'

Without waiting for an answer she shut the door.

Rawson went back to his car, started the engine and drove far enough down the road for him to be out of sight from Norden's aunt. In his inside pocket was a mass of old letters that he had pushed there and forgotten; he took them out now and sorted through them until he found the one he wanted, an official-looking circular from the police, telling him of a lorry load of cameras which had been stolen and which might be offered to him cheaply.

One of the items listed was a carton containing twenty-five Minolta cameras. This was the carton that he had seen in the hall of the bungalow.

15

Carton

There could be no doubt about it. The carton had been well away from the front door, and half hidden by a pile of old clothes, but the name had been visible, Minolta, in large red letters, with Japanese symbols beneath it. One thing was certain; it wasn't full of cameras now, but old newspapers. Of course it could have been come by normally, through Roxy's warehouse; that was the simple explanation.

He let in the clutch and moved off. He would go to Jean's and have some lunch and then go and see Norden's aunt in Watford.

He was soon at the flat, and after parking his car he ran up the stairs and along the newly painted corridor. Almost as soon as he had rung the bell he heard the sound of footsteps from inside the flat, then the noise of someone drawing back a bolt.

The door opened and he saw Jean.

She said: 'Brian, thank goodness you've come.'

For a moment he didn't speak or move, then he stepped into the flat. 'What's the matter?' he asked.

'Nothing at the moment,' she answered, following him in. 'There's no one here or anything like that.'

She shut the door and told him to sit down, sitting opposite to him in one of the easy chairs. 'It's Mike really, he seems to be acting so oddly.'

'What else has he done?'

Rawson sensed the girl's tautness and stretched out his legs, trying to give an impression of relaxed ease in the hope that it would calm her.

She twisted her fingers together. 'There was the way he carried on when you were here,' she began, 'but it really started last night. I didn't expect him back so soon, for a start.'

'Why did he come back?'

'He says that he finished the business

149

that he went to do.' Jean shrugged. 'It could be true or it could be something he's made up.'

'Is he really your fiancé?' Rawson asked as she paused.

She hesitated. 'No,' she said at length. 'I — I'd like him to be. That's why it would be so awful if he was mixed up in this. Last night I told him that I was worried about Sonia and all he did at the end of it was try and make love to me as if he didn't care at all about how I felt.' Her voice rose, and Rawson sensed that hysterics were not far away. 'I stopped him and he seemed to realise then that I was bothered about her, but — ' She broke off. 'He is acting so oddly,' she finished.

Rawson moved slowly, keeping up his attitude of relaxed ease. 'Has he ever done anything like this before?'

'No.'

'Where is he now?'

'He says that he's gone to his office.'

Rawson said: 'You can settle that right away. Ring him and ask him something. Say you've forgotten what time he said he'd be back.'

Jean stood up, crossed to the phone and dialled quickly, waiting only a few seconds before she asked for Mike. After a short conversation she hung up.

'He's there all right.'

'So at least we know that some of the things he said are true,' Rawson commented. He would have to be very careful here if Jean really did love Cartney. He said slowly: 'How many pairs of shoes has Sonia got with that letter 'S' stitched on the toe?'

'Only one. An American firm that she modelled them for gave them to her about two months ago. Why?'

Still speaking slowly, he said: 'I found one by Roxy's body.'

She drew breath sharply. 'Oh, Lord! But you didn't tell Heaton?' There was a question in her voice.

'No.' He stood up. 'Could you have a look if the other one is here anywhere?'

'Of course.' Jean went into the bedroom, and for some minutes there came the sound of things being moved, drawers opened and closed, then she

151

came back. 'No,' she said. 'Both of the shoes are missing.'

'So, at least we know that she had them on,' Rawson commented, not wanting to tell her his suspicions of Cartney, unfounded as it seemed. To change the subject quickly he said: 'Do you or Sonia know anyone called Harry Spencer?'

'No.' She sat down again, smoothing her skirt with one hand. 'I'm quite certain of that.'

Quickly, he told her what had happened at Roxy's, and then went on to mention the camera carton at Norden's.

'So it looks as if Norden and Harry Spencer are the people we're looking for,' he finished. 'I don't know whether or not to tell Heaton. After all, it does help to take his attention off Sonia, doesn't it?'

Jean said: 'The shoe doesn't.'

'Need we mention that? He already thinks that I'm holding something back. It should satisfy him if I tell him about Norden and Spencer.'

She shook her head quickly. 'No it won't. When he thought you were holding something back he knew that you hadn't been to Roxy's. If you tell him something now that you could only have found out after you left him this morning it'll only make it more suspicious. I should say nothing. After all, he can't prove anything.'

Rawson thought quickly, seeing the sense of Jean's reasoning.

'You can't explain the phone calls?' he asked hopefully.

'No.' Most of the nervousness had gone now. Once she had something to think about other than the fact that Cartney might be involved it was remarkable how quickly she calmed down. 'What did Wesloe have to say?'

'He rejected most of the ideas I put to him.' Rawson gave her a summary of the conversation, then stood up.

'I'll have to get back to my place soon. I'll send my assistant over to keep an eye on you, and ask him to ring me if anything looks like going wrong. How will that do?'

'That'll be fine.'

All the emotion that she had shown

before had collapsed now; if anything she was more tired than hysterical.

★ ★ ★

While Rawson was at Jean's, Superintendent Heaton sat in his office at the Yard. The only sound in the room was the noise of the typewriter as Field typed some reports ready for the Commander, who would be sure to want them when he came in after lunch.

Suddenly Heaton said: 'Geoff, where's that list we had from Southampton? The stolen cameras.'

Field stopped typing, shuffled through his papers on the desk and passed two thin sheets across to Heaton, who glanced at them before laying them down in front of him.

The robbery had taken place some three weeks before, near Southampton. A lorry, loaded with nearly ten thousand pounds' worth of cameras had been stopped on a lonely road. The driver had been coshed, bundled out of the cab, and the lorry driven off. There had been no trace of the cameras since, although the empty lorry and the tracks of another vehicle, to which the cameras must have been transferred, had been found in a country lane near by. The local police had circulated particulars, expecting that at least some of the cameras would be offered through the usual channels, and that sooner or later a police force somewhere would get some information, but there had been nothing.

Heaton reached out for the phone, and asked for the Southampton number.

Field said: 'Is it any more certain that there's a connection?'

'It might be,' Heaton said drily. 'What do you think?'

Before Field had time to answer the call came through. Heaton asked for Superintendent Lucas and waited for the connection to be made.

'Mr. Lucas? Chief Superintendent Heaton of Scotland Yard here. Heard any more about those cameras?'

'Not a thing,' Lucas answered in a strong Northern accent. 'Have you got something?' There was a faint trace of hope in his voice.

'I may have, but it's only at the idea stage at the moment. I've a missing model and two photographers. It would tie in very neatly.'

'Too neatly,' the Southampton man commented. 'Probably nothing in it.'

'What makes you say that?'

'I'm tired,' Lucas answered at once. 'I've been working on this case for nearly a month. I gave up thinking there'd be an easy solution long ago. Let me know if you do get anything, won't you?'

Heaton rang off and leaned back, the list still in front of him. 'Has anything at all been found at Roxy's place that could be connected with these?'

Field shook his head. 'The only odd thing so far is that bloodstain.'

Heaton pursed his lips. The bloodstain had been on the floor of Roxy's studio, not far from the body. At first it had been assumed that it was Roxy's blood, but further checking had disproved this. That only left the model; if she had attacked Roxy and had been hurt in the ensuing struggle, it would be explained very easily.

On the other hand, to have left a stain so big she would have had to lose a lot of blood and would have been certain to have collapsed not long afterwards.

So she might be dead after all.

The phone rang again; Heaton, toying with various ideas, let it shrill until Field moved to answer. Heaton shook his head and reached out.

'Heaton.'

'Hello, John. Doing any good on Shaftesbury Avenue?' The caller was Mossop, a Divisional Inspector.

'I may be,' Heaton answered cautiously, then went on:

'Found that copper of yours who called on Jean Dixon last night?'

'Yes.'

'You have?' There was surprise in Heaton's voice. 'What did he want?'

'We don't mess around in this Division, you know,' Mossop replied, almost smugly, then his voice hardened. 'You won't like it, John.'

'Try me.'

'He was being blackmailed. Apparently Roxy had some hold over him, I'm not sure what yet. Last night he got a message, through Bradford, that Roxy wanted him to call round at the flat and ask for Sonia Dixon. He doesn't know why.'

He paused.

'Silly young fool,' Heaton commented. 'Could cost him his job. Depends what this hold is, and what else he's done.'

'Apart from that, he's one of my best lads,' Mossop said. 'Never can tell, John. There's another thing, too.'

'What's that?'

'A report from one of my chaps who was near Roxy's last night at about eight o'clock. While he was there he saw a man whom he remembered from a case last year, chap named Harry Spencer. He was with two other men, who might have been his two brothers. My fellow isn't sure of that.'

'Know their names?' Heaton asked, scribbling on his pad.

'No.'

'Soon find out,' Heaton grunted. 'Thanks, Bill.'

He hung up and passed the scribbled

notes across to Field.

'Can you nip to Records and see what they've got on Spencer and his brothers?'

Field took the paper and left the room.

He wasn't long before he came back; there was no smile on his face, although a gleam in his eyes showed that he had found out something which he thought would surprise Heaton. He let the door swing shut after him, then crossed quickly to Heaton's desk, a number of photos in his hand.

He laid them on the desk.

'Spencer, his elder brother Cliff and his younger brother, Tom, known as Blackie,' he said, pointing them out.

'Why Blackie?' Heaton asked.

'Because he likes to wear black things. You know, black jeans, black leather jacket and so on.' Field still held a photo. 'This is something that's come in for identification.'

He laid the picture alongside the others. It showed the head and shoulders of a man, obviously dead. Heaton gazed at it, then scrutinised the others.

'There isn't much doubt, is there?'

'None, I'd say,' Field answered. 'The deado is Blackie Spencer.'

After a number of phone calls, there was no doubt at all. Not only was the deado Blackie Spencer, but his blood group matched the stain on Roxy's floor.

'What do you make of it?' Field asked.

'I'm not sure. Try this. Assuming the stolen cameras are involved, I'd say they were stolen by Spencer and his cronies, and that they planned to get rid of them through Roxy. There was some kind of quarrel. Roxy was killed and Blackie Spencer was injured.'

'Why send the copper to Jean Dixon?'

'Because Sonia was involved with Roxy. Either that or she's working with Rawson. Whichever way it is, there's some reason why she has to hide. If she just vanished, Jean would go to the police. The best way of stopping her is to send the police to her.'

He stopped and frowned.

'I think that lets Rawson out,' he said slowly.

'How come?'

'Well, if Rawson hadn't been there,

we'd never have known anything about Jean or Sonia. The picture would have looked like this. Roxy would have been killed. We'd have investigated that. Sonia would have run off, but we wouldn't have known anything about that because this copper would have stopped Jean from going to the police. We might have found out about the quarrel between Roxy and Sonia, or we might not have done.' He shrugged. 'It looks to me as though it would have worked if Rawson hadn't happened along.'

'And what about this Norden who worked for Roxy?'

'There's that to look into,' Heaton agreed. 'I'm still not entirely happy about Rawson. I have the feeling he's hiding something.' He pressed his lips together. 'What I'd like to do is prove that Sonia Dixon was at Roxy's. If I could do that I reckon we'd be on the way to cracking this case.'

16

Janet Models

This was the moment when Rawson arrived back at his studio after leaving Jean's flat. He had stopped once on the way, to ring Pam Woods from a call box, and tell her that Norden had spent the night at Watford. As he walked from the car to the studio now, he wondered what he was going to do about Norden, and about the camera carton that he had seen at the bungalow. The obvious thing was to go to Watford, but there was no guarantee of finding anything even if he did, and there must by now be a considerable list of appointments that he had already missed that day.

He tried to remember who had been coming.

No one really important as far as he could recall. He wondered what Janet had told them, tried to imagine her soothing a waiting-room full of seething clients. He drove as fast as he could, but found only Janet in the reception room when he got there. She looked up as she heard him come in.

'Where have you been?'

'Having a bit of trouble with the police.' He dropped into one of the easy chairs. 'Roxy was murdered last night.'

'Roxy?'

'Yes. I found the body.'

Janet said: 'Oh!'

'Is there a paper handy?'

'No. We don't get a morning one at home and I'm always in too much of a hurry to call for one. Why?'

'I just wanted to see if there was anything in it, that's all.' He glanced towards the door at the back of the room. 'Where's Bill?'

'He's in the studio. Do you want him?' As Rawson nodded she picked up the phone, pushed over the switch that would connect it with the studio and pressed the button that rang the bell.

They heard it ring faintly and a minute later she asked Bill to come in.

Rawson watched her, getting a sudden impression that there was something odd about her manner, something other than the effect that hearing of the murder would have on her. More an air of suppressed excitement than anything else, he thought.

The door opened and Bill came in. He looked surprised when he saw Rawson and then asked bluntly:

'Have you heard about Roxy?'

'Yes. Bill, I want you to do something that doesn't strictly come into your job. I want you to go and keep watch on a flat and ring me if you think that there's any reason why I should be there. It may mean staying rather late, so if you don't want to do it say so.'

Bill didn't hesitate. Almost grinning, as if that was the thing he wanted to do most of all, he said: 'I'll do it. Will you be coming along later anyway?'

'I'll come after tea,' Rawson said, not really sure if it would be wise to go while Cartney was there. 'If I'm not coming I'll ring you and tell you to go home.' He gave Bill the address and told him to ring the bell and let Jean know he was there.

The lad went out of the door.

Janet said: 'What's the matter at Jean's?'

'Nothing, I hope. It's just that she thinks that Cartney may have something to do with Sonia's disappearance.' He smiled faintly. 'Of course, Cartney's convinced that I planned it all, so really it doesn't help us much.'

Janet ran her fingers over the typewriter keys, making a faint tinkling noise.

Rawson asked about the clients.

'I told them you were ill. When it got to eleven o'clock and you still hadn't come back I rang up the ones who were due this afternoon and told them you wouldn't be in. Most of them fixed fresh appointments. Mrs. Tate more or less hung up on me and that man Nicholson who wanted those portraits of his son said he'd think about it.'

Rawson nodded. The lost business didn't really matter; there was normally much more than he could cope with.

'So we've got a free day?'

'That's right.'

He stood up and moved towards the camera room, intending to check that everything was all right in there before locking it up and concentrating on finding the missing Dick Norden.

He was conscious of Janet following him along the corridor.

They went into the camera room. She shut the door then hurried so that she was in front of him, blocking his path.

'Has Bill said anything to you about me and some photos?'

Rawson hesitated, annoyed with himself because he hadn't foreseen that, with the rest of the day free, this might happen.

'He — '

'Has he?' she demanded.

'Yes, but — '

'But you don't think I'm good enough?'

She stood in front of him, wearing a short-sleeved black dress.

Was she good enough?

In this dress she didn't look as well built as he had thought, in fact she looked quite slim. Her face was expressive enough too; he might be able to do something after all. Before he had time to say anything she reached behind her with one hand and slowly unzipped the dress. She gave a little seductive wriggle, leaning forward so that the dress fell away from her breasts then slid to the floor. Still looking at Rawson, she stepped away from it.

She wore the briefest white bikini, trimmed with black.

She was at least as lovely as any model he had ever used.

'Well?'

She raised herself on to her toes, lifted one hand to pat her hair, then turned slowly right round until she was facing him again.

'Well?' she repeated. 'Am I as good as the others?'

She came very close to him, so close that he wanted to reach out and take her shoulders to stop her. With an effort he kept his hands at his side; to touch her in the mood she was in might lead to endless trouble.

'Yes, Janet,' he said as she stopped walking. 'You're every bit as good.'

She smiled faintly.

'But you won't photograph me? I'll pay you if you want.' She added the last words a little bitterly.

Rawson rubbed his ear slowly.

She backed away a pace.

'You think I'm no good, don't you, Brian? You think I won't do what you ask me to? Well I will! I'll do anything that Sonia Dixon ever did!'

With a quick movement, she stripped off the top of the bikini, throwing it to the floor. She raised herself on to her toes again. With an effort Rawson looked into her eyes; he saw them widen slightly, as at something behind him which he couldn't see. The door was behind him. He turned, hearing a faint noise as he did so.

A young man stood there dressed in black jeans and a short leather jacket, also black. He walked up to Rawson, thumbs hooked into his belt, staring at him.

He said: 'I've got something to put to you, Rawson.'

17

Proposition

He stepped farther into the room, taking no notice of Janet, who moved back, hands crossed in front of her.

Rawson said: 'Who are you?', although he guessed that he could only be the missing Norden.

'My name's Norden, for what it matters. Are you going to listen to me or not?'

'That depends on what you've got to say.'

'You think you're smart, don't you, Rawson?'

He stood squarely in front of Rawson, his hands clenched. At twenty-three, Norden had had five jobs since leaving school in Bedford, where he had lived and where his parents still lived, before coming to the 'smoke'. He thought that he would have better prospects of the sort of job he wanted in London, and had stayed with an aunt. For almost a year he had worked in a garage, and then he had replied to Roxy's advert in the paper. He didn't really know why at the time; he wasn't specially interested in photography and, at the resulting interview, he hadn't known what to answer to most of the questions. To his surprise Roxy had offered him the job, with higher wages and better conditions than he had had at the garage.

He had started as Roxy's assistant. At the back of his mind had been the thought that he might get to know some models, but he had soon realised that they weren't interested in someone who was just an assistant and who had hardly any money. The only girl who had shown any interest in him at all had been Pam Woods, who had come to work there as a receptionist about three months after he had started; now, he was taking her out more from desperation than because he liked her.

The work he did at Roxy's had become more and more fascinating to him, until he believed that he had at last found a job to which he could settle. At work he dressed quietly, almost soberly, but now he was wearing what he called his gear; jeans, a heavy sweater with red bands across the chest, and a worn leather jacket with the make of his motor scooter painted in white across the back.

Still the models would take no notice of him . . .

Then he thought that he had found a way to make the kind of money he needed. An easy way. He had seen what Roxy kept hidden in one of his storerooms, and had spoken to him about it.

Blackmail was such an easy way to make big money.

Then had come the happenings on the night of Roxy's murder which had led him eventually to Rawson.

'You think you're smart, don't you?' he repeated, sneering.

Rawson said: 'Calm down. I don't think anything at the moment. I may do if you protest too much.'

'What do you mean?' Norden moved

171

forward a pace and Rawson involuntarily stepped back. Out of the corner of his eye he could see Janet watching him anxiously; Norden's movements meant that he now had one heel on the hem of her dress and that if she moved to pick up the top of the bikini she would step right into his line of vision. Rawson's lip twitched. In spite of the fact that he felt it was her own fault he had to help her.

'Sit down,' he said curtly to Norden.

There was a chair in front of the young man; if he sat in it he wouldn't see Janet until she had had a chance to reach her clothes.

'Why?' Norden shouted the word.

'Sit down!'

This time, instead of answering, Norden lunged forward. Rawson sidestepped and Norden pivoted quickly on one heel, his fist striking out again.

He saw Janet. His mouth gaped, then it closed and he set his lips firmly.

'So that's how you pass your time while your girlfriend's missing, is it?'

'Are you going to sit down?'

'In a minute,' Norden was still eyeing

Janet, who was picking up her dress, half turned away from him. 'Don't be shy, chick,' he urged. 'Let's have a look at you.'

Rawson took hold of his shoulders, twisted him away from her and pushed him into the chair. He resisted slightly, then sat back, watching Janet as, holding the dress in front of her, she went into the changing room.

As the door closed behind her, Rawson said: 'Now tell me what you're after and what you know about Sonia.'

Now that he was sitting Norden had to look up at him.

'Sonia? I know plenty about Sonia.' Traces of the sneer were still in his voice. 'For instance, I know that she didn't kill that jerk, Roxy.'

'How do you know that?' Rawson's voice sharpened.

'Because I know who did kill him, that's how. It wasn't the chick.'

'Have you seen Pam Woods recently?'

Norden stared. 'Her!' he spat contemptuously. 'No.'

'Then you don't know that you're one

173

of the main suspects?'

'But I'm not!' Norden burst out. 'I wasn't even — '

He broke off abruptly, his eyes drifting to the changing room door as it opened and Janet came out. She barely glanced at the two men as she passed through the room. Rawson was tempted to call her back, but he let her go, realising that she would be useful in the reception room for keeping out anyone else who might try to get in.

Norden said: 'I never remember seeing her around. Who is she?'

'Never mind her. Let's get back to Roxy. How do you know who killed him?'

Norden didn't answer the question. He said: 'They tell me you found the body?'

'Who tells you?'

'The papers, if you must know. How did you find him? You weren't one of his pals. What made you go round there at that time?'

'You should know that, you seem to know everything else,' Rawson snapped. 'Look, I haven't got time to waste — '

'You went looking for the chick, didn't

you? Listen, Rawson, I know where she is. I know who killed Roxy and I know where they are too. If you knew that, it'd put you off the hook, wouldn't it?'

'What do you mean by that?'

Norden grinned unpleasantly. 'What I say. You went round there for the first time just after he was killed. The police must think that's pretty odd, mustn't they?'

'Perhaps they do. I've told you, you're the main suspect.' All the time he was speaking, thoughts of the carton of cameras were at the back of his mind, but he decided to let Norden say what he had to say before he mentioned it, then see what happened.

'Suppose I told you where she was,' Norden was saying now. 'How much would it be worth to you?'

'You're trying to blackmail me?'

'Not blackmail, pal. Just trying to pass on a bit of gen, that's all. Blackmail's an ugly word.'

'What you're doing is ugly,' Rawson replied. 'If I don't pay, you push off and I'm no nearer finding Sonia, even though she's innocent. Is she with the killer?' He fired the last question abruptly, hoping to catch Norden off his guard.

'No pay, no gen,' Norden stated flatly.

'What makes you try this stunt? Have you fallen out with your pals or something?'

'They're no pals of mine. I just want a bit of money, that's all.'

'How did you find out all this?'

'I was there,' answered Norden surprisingly. 'I was across the road when they came out. None of them saw me; I put two and two together afterwards. It wasn't hard.'

'What are you going to do if I throw you out?'

Norden hesitated.

Rawson pressed the argument. 'If what you say is true, they won't be able to find the real killers without finding Sonia. Why should I pay you?'

Norden looked at him sullenly. 'You still think you're being smart, don't you, Rawson? Listen, pal, let me tell you a few things. Roxy often used to have women in his flat during the day. He was like that.

Most of his women were models, too; he used to tell the new ones that he could help them if they'd sleep with him. A few of them were thick enough to fall for it. If I tell the cops Sonia was one of them, that she was mad at him for letting her down, they'll guess that she went round there to argue with him, and then killed him.'

'Sonia hated him.'

'Of course she did,' Norden replied blandly. 'That's what I'm telling you. Because she hated him she went round and killed him.'

'Suppose I agree to pay you,' Rawson said mildly. 'What do you do then?'

'I give you the gen and push off. You don't see me again.'

'How can I be sure you're telling the truth?'

'You'll have to take my word for it.'

'Take your word!' Rawson laughed. 'No chance. In any case, what is your price?'

'Five thousand quid.'

'Suppose I haven't got it?'

'Tough. You don't get the gen.'

'Then you don't get any money.

There's no one else you can sell to, you know.'

Norden was silent, sitting in his chair, looking up at him defiantly.

Rawson said: 'Just one more question.'

'What's that?'

'What's that carton of Minoltas doing at your aunt's?'

Norden started, half rising from his chair.

'Sit down!'

Rawson pushed him back, but as soon as he let go Norden bobbed up again, his fists striking out. Rawson stepped back a pace, so that the blows fell short and then moved in before Norden had had time to recover. He took hold of one of his arms, bending it, twisting it down and over the chair arm. The pressure pulled Norden partly out of his seat; his free arm waved wildly, but Rawson was well out of reach.

Norden gasped with pain.

Rawson gave the arm a final twist before releasing it.

'Now tell me about the cameras,' he suggested. 'Suppose I go to the police with that? Where does it leave you then?'

'You wouldn't.'

'Why not?' He stopped speaking as there was a soft tap on the door. It opened and Janet came in.

She said to Rawson: 'Superintendent Heaton is here. He wants to see you right away.'

18

Dilemma

Thoughts ran swiftly through Rawson's mind, then, through the silence which seemed to have clamped round him, he heard Janet ask: 'Are you all right?'

He shook himself irritably. He mustn't show reaction as easily as this, especially with the police about waiting to pounce on anything he did which might seem suspicious.

'Sorry, Jan, I was thinking of something else. Must he see me right away?'

'So he says.'

'Tell him I'll be along in a moment.'

When she had gone out he turned to Norden.

Norden stated flatly: 'If the cops get me you'll never see Sonia again.'

This was one of the thoughts in Rawson's own mind. He needed to keep Norden to himself for the moment, to see him at leisure and force him to tell what he knew.

He pointed to a door.

'That's one of the dressing-rooms. If you stay in there until I come back you should be all right.'

Without answering, Norden went into the room, shutting the door softly.

Rawson hurried to the reception room. Heaton was sitting in a chair as far away from Janet's desk as he could get, but whether this was deliberate or whether that had been the handiest chair, Rawson couldn't tell. As he went into the room, Heaton stood up.

'Good morning, Mr. Rawson.'

'Good morning. Will this take long?'

'Why?' He made even the simple question into a menacing thing, almost an accusation.

'I'm busy. I've a lot of work to get through today.'

'I quite appreciate your point,' Heaton answered urbanely. 'I trust that you can spare me a few minutes?'

Rawson nodded, conscious that behind the man's easy, genial manner there was a

181

certain deadliness that would have to be watched for, found and avoided, not only now but later when he would be more off guard.

The Yard man gestured faintly towards Janet; the sign was almost unnoticeable. 'You're willing to talk, Mr. Rawson?'

'Quite willing. Whatever you've got to say you can say here.'

'Thank you.' Heaton paused, weighing his facts. 'When did you last see Sonia Dixon?'

'The day before yesterday.'

'What time did she leave?'

'About three o'clock. She was due back at half past ten yesterday.'

'Just answer the questions, Mr. Rawson. Could she have gone to Roxy's after leaving here?'

'She could have done.' This was the first of the barbed questions. 'Why?'

'I just want to know. It might have some bearing on my investigations.'

'Look, Mr. Heaton, I don't know what you're getting at, but if Sonia went to Roxy's it was because she had an appointment there. If that was the case, two things would have happened. She would have mentioned it to me because she knew that I was aware of the situation between her and Roxy, and it will be in his appointment book or hers.'

Heaton said: 'What was the situation between him and Miss Dixon? I know she didn't like him, but just what did Roxy think of her?'

'I don't know.'

'What I'm trying to get at is this, Mr. Rawson. Would he have been likely to think that her attitude was due to pride on her part? The feeling that now she'd reached the top he wasn't good enough for her? Would he have been likely to want to teach her a lesson?'

'Teach her a lesson?' Rawson actually laughed at the absurdity of the thought. In a way, this was good, as it eased the tension both in himself and in the room.

'Mr. Heaton, Roxy was a grown man, he didn't go about teaching people lessons. Perhaps it would be a good idea if you told me exactly what you want to know. I might be able to help you then, instead of just sitting here fencing with you.'

For what seemed like minutes, Heaton was silent; at length he said: 'I went round to Roxy's again earlier today. While I was there I made a thorough examination of the whole place and I found one or two odd things. I found a lockable trunk, for example. It was in the studio, where Roxy's body was, and at some stage the lock had been forced. On the sides of the trunk, inside, there were marks that could only have been made by one thing: a woman's high-heeled shoe kicking against the wood.'

'So?'

'So I want to know if the woman could have been Sonia Dixon, locked in the trunk by Roxy to teach her a lesson and so angry when he finally released her that she grabbed the first thing she saw, a knife, and killed him.'

Rawson's hands clenched, partly at the thought of Sonia locked in the trunk, and partly at Heaton's reasoning.

'Is it likely that the first thing she would grab would be a knife?'

'Could be. There were a few lying around. Sharp, too; wouldn't take much force to stab with them.'

'Don't you think that she would be so cramped and exhausted when he let her out that she would have no strength to grab anything?'

'That could be,' Heaton admitted reluctantly. At one stage, when he had first known of the truth, he had considered asking a policewoman to try the test to see what state she was in when he let her out, but he was reluctant to ask any girl, even a volunteer, to submit to the ordeal of being squashed into that locked trunk, with no idea when she was going to be released. There were other factors, of course, that would make such a test nothing more than a rough guess; he didn't know how long Sonia had been locked up, and he didn't know how terrified she had been. That in itself would take a lot out of her, but on the other hand he knew that some of these models had lengthy powers of endurance.

He said. 'There's only one other point,

Mr. Rawson. Do you know a man named Harry Spencer?'

That was the name that the man had said at Roxy's.

Rawson hesitated fractionally before answering: 'Should I?'

'Not really.' Heaton shrugged, then smiled as he had got what he had really come for. He turned and went to the door. 'Good day, Mr. Rawson.'

As he closed the door, Janet looked up from the filing she had been doing during the conversation, then came out from behind the desk, her eyes clouded.

'Brian, I'm sorry.'

'For what?'

'For what happened before. And for what I said about Sonia. Can we forget it?'

He leaned over and kissed her lightly on her upturned forehead. 'We can't do that,' he declared. 'No beautiful girl who does what you've just done can expect a man to forget it, just like that.'

She blushed.

'Let me sort this business out, then we'll see what we can do,' he promised, moving towards the door. 'I'd better sort Norden out.'

Janet said: 'There is one other thing.'

'What's that?'

She went back behind her desk and took something from one of the drawers.

'When I got back here after Norden had arrived, this was on the desk. I didn't want to interrupt you while you were with him, though.'

She handed him a plain brown envelope, which seemed to be very bulky. He fingered it, and realised that most of the bulkiness came from the thickness of the paper; whatever was inside it wasn't very big. He slit it open with his thumb, parted the ragged edges and looked inside. There was a single sheet of paper, folded once, which proved to be a cutting from a magazine.

It was a colour picture of Sonia, head and shoulders.

She looked beautiful on it, except for the vivid red scars on her face.

19

Scars

There were two scars in the cutting, both so well done that they seemed to be part of the original photo. It was only when he turned the picture to the light, tilting it slightly so that the light fell diagonally on it, that he could see how they had been put on with a red ballpoint pen. One of them ran across her forehead, the other from ear to ear under her chin.

Janet breathed: 'Why, it's — it's wicked!'

'It is,' Rawson agreed grimly. 'When did this come?'

'While I was in there with you. I found it when I came back, but there was nothing to show who'd brought it in.'

'Was the door open all the time?'

'It was unlocked, yes.'

Rawson grunted. Anyone could have walked in, dropped the envelope on

Janet's desk and walked out again. He wondered for a brief moment if Norden could have done it as he passed through the reception room, but there was no reason why he should have done. Why, if it had been him, should he leave it on the desk, where it wouldn't be found until he had gone? Why not give it to him personally, as a kind of warning as to what might happen to Sonia if he didn't pay?

He dropped the cutting on to the desk.

'Don't throw it away,' he said in a flat voice. 'It might be needed later on.'

'What are you going to do?'

Rawson asked: 'Do you think she killed Roxy?'

'Of course not! I think that she was there when he was killed and she's been kidnapped because of that.'

He nodded, then forced himself to say: 'In that case, why kidnap her? Why not kill her right away?'

Janet drew breath. 'You don't think — '

He shook his head impatiently. 'No. If they had killed her there wouldn't be any point in sending this photo. I think that she's going to be used as a lever against me. That would explain several things. The phone calls to the Press and to Wesloe's, for a start. This photo, too, to show me what they could do to her if I didn't play ball.'

'But why should they want a lever against you?'

'I've no idea. Wesloe's come to mind, but that's too farfetched. Let me go and have another word with Norden.'

Leaving Janet where she was, he went to the studio, thoughtfully, where he found that Norden had left the dressing-room and was inspecting a camera set up on a tripod.

'He's gone,' Rawson said.

'The cop! Good. Have you thought about what I said?'

'A little.' Rawson showed him the photo. 'Know anything about this?'

The young man sucked in his breath with a loud hiss; it was evident from his surprise that he had never seen the picture before. Rawson tucked it back into his pocket.

'When did that come?' Norden demanded.

'Just after you.'

'I don't know anything about it — '

'Perhaps not.' Without warning Rawson stepped forward and grabbed Norden's arm. 'What do you know about Harry Spencer?'

'About — '

'Harry Spencer.'

Rawson felt a surge of joy. Norden had looked startled, too startled to be able to deny successfully that he didn't know Spencer was involved.

'Come off it, Norden.' Rawson twisted the arm that he held. For a moment Norden didn't resist, then he began to struggle. He was smaller than Rawson, but he had a tough, wiry strength and the suddenness of his attack let him succeed for a short time. Rawson managed to hold on to him and dragged him across the floor farther into the room.

'It is Spencer, isn't it?'

He let go of Norden's arm and pushed him backwards. He stumbled a few steps before saving himself

'All right,' he said in a low voice. 'All right.'

Rawson went up to him, taking a fistful of shirt and almost lifting the lad off his feet. 'Well?'

'He's involved.'

'What do you know about this business?'

'Not much.' Norden squirmed. 'You're choking me.'

Rawson dropped him; he thought that Norden was going to make a dash for the door, but he didn't move.

Slowly, he began to tell what he knew.

'I wanted money,' he said softly. 'It's no joke trying to live in London on a low wage, but there was nothing I could do about it until I found all those cameras in Roxy's storeroom. I got it out of him that he'd nicked them, and started to put the black on him. He paid me once, then when I went to see him the other night for a touch, I saw some blokes going in. I knew one of them was Spencer, because Roxy had told me about him, so I waited for a heck of a time before they came out. When they did, there was a girl with them, unconscious. I watched them put her in a van, then load all the cameras in after her. When they drove off I followed them, then I went home. When I read about Roxy in the papers I knew what had happened.'

He paused.

'Go on,' Rawson prompted grimly.

'I went round to where they were.' Norden gulped. 'I tried to put the black on Spencer, but he wouldn't have any of it, so I came here.'

He paused again, and Rawson grinned. He guessed that Spencer was a hardened crook and could visualise exactly what his reaction would have been when a kid like Norden came to try and blackmail him. Most of the plot was revealed now; the things that remained could be cleared up when he had got Spencer.

He asked: 'Where is Spencer now?'

'I've no idea.' Norden looked at him defiantly.

'Come off it. Where was he when you went to see him?'

'For God's sake! If you went there with the cops and he got away, he'd know that it was me who sent you. He'd kill me! You can't make me tell you!'

'Can't I? Don't forget that Sonia's involved in this. As far as I'm concerned it isn't just a matter of these stolen cameras.' A thought came to him. 'I suppose you got that boxful off Roxy.'

'That's right.' Norden's voice was low and sullen now. 'I thought that it'd be a bit of extra money. I couldn't sell them, though. They're still at my aunt's, hidden in my room.'

'Where's Spencer?' Rawson asked.

Norden licked his lips; before he answered the phone rang suddenly, shrilly. Rawson glanced towards it and Norden took his chance. Pushing Rawson violently in the chest, he dragged himself free and raced across the floor.

Janet —

If she tried to stop him —

He saw Norden open the door and dash into the passage. He was too far away now for Rawson to reach him before he was in the street; the faint sound of running footsteps came to him, then a murmur of voices, followed by a sharp cry from Janet.

The phone was still ringing.

He hurried to the door. Janet was in the passage, standing on one foot and supporting herself with one arm on the wall. She was rubbing her leg, lips pursed, breath hissing.

'Are you all right?'

She looked up. 'I think so. I tried to stop him, but he kicked me. He caught me on the shin and by the time I could think again he'd gone.'

The phone was ringing dully and insistently. There was no hope of catching Norden now, so he turned back to the studio.

Janet said: 'It's switched through.'

Rawson nodded. He went into the studio and picked up the receiver.

★   ★   ★

In a room about three miles away, Sonia Dixon stood by the phone. The man who held her had his arm tightly round her shoulders; this pressed the collar of the heavy man's coat she wore up around her

195

ears so that she could only hear faintly what was said. She had struggled to try to break the hold, but the man had hit her once; after that she had remained still.

She tried to hear what he was saying into the phone, realising that it must concern her or he wouldn't have brought her here.

She heard him say: 'Do you want to see Sonia again, Rawson?'

There was a pause, then came the words: 'You'd better do as I say. Listen, Rawson.'

The pressure of his arm increased suddenly. Startled, she looked up. The light glittered on a knife blade; it shone as it plunged towards her.

She screamed.

Rawson heard the scream.

It was followed by a click as the man hung up. As he replaced his own receiver, he thought about what the man had said. If you want to see Sonia again you'd better do as I say. He had gone on to say that he wanted to talk to Rawson and given him an address, that of a restaurant in Limehouse, where he was to come at three o'clock.

It was half past one now.

He hurried back to the reception-room.

20

Trouble for Norden

Meanwhile, after leaving Rawson's, Dick Norden walked quickly, thinking what a fool he had been ever to get involved in this. At first it had seemed a good idea to go to Roxy and tell him that unless he paid he would tell the police. Roxy had kicked at first, naturally, but he had come round to Norden's way of thinking. On the day of the killing Norden had been off work; he had gone to see Roxy that night, when he knew that there would be no clients to disturb them, to get some more money from him.

He had seen the Spencers, two of them, and a third man, a stranger.

It had seemed a good idea to try to blackmail them too, but when he had gone to see them he had found them far tougher than Roxy.

He knew that if he wasn't careful they

would kill him. Money was essential now, if only to get out of London, back to Bedford where he thought he would be safe. It was all Roxy's fault, he told himself. If Roxy had never allowed himself to be talked into pinching the cameras in the first place, he couldn't have been blackmailed and there wouldn't be this mess now.

Feelings of hate against everybody filled Norden; he walked quickly.

* * *

Behind him, unnoticed, walked Constable Wheeler. He was in plain clothes, acting as an Aid-to-CID before actually being transferred to that branch. He had come to Rawson's with Heaton, and had been told to wait outside. When Heaton returned he had told Wheeler to stay there and follow anyone who came out.

Wheeler had waited in a doorway farther along. He had been thinking of his garden.

Three months ago he had been married and had moved to a house with a large garden, the only one left of three on a new housing estate. It was only just within their price range, but Diane, his wife, had been so insistent on a new house that he had bought it. His parents' house had no garden, so he had never done any gardening before; now, the size of this garden was proving to be more of a problem than he had imagined. Quite apart from the physical work of digging all the ground, which didn't really worry him, there was the question of filling it with flowers.

He would have to do something soon. He was due for some leave the following week, and Diane had persuaded him to make a start then.

He thought of the problems of the garden as he waited, finding CID work much duller than he had imagined.

He could fill a lot of the garden with a lawn, of course, although he wanted a big one at the back where they were sheltered from the other houses by some trees. They could sunbathe there in the summer; he was looking forward to that. If he put lawns at the front and back though, it would surround the house with grass; far too much grass.

It was quite a problem for someone who had never had a garden before. He was still thinking about it when Norden came out of Rawson's and hurried off.

Wheeler followed.

The garden would have to wait.

★ ★ ★

Norden, intent on his own thoughts, didn't notice that he was being followed. He bumped into one or two people, mumbling apologies, and began to walk slower and slower.

He didn't think that he was in any danger yet.

He didn't see the van until it was far too late.

The pavement was not as crowded here as it had been and there was only himself and another man, who wasn't very far away. The van leapt towards him, swinging on to the pavement. Norden threw up one arm, trying to ward it off, but it caught him squarely and threw him into the air.

A woman screamed.

Behind him, Wheeler's mouth opened and, oblivious of danger to himself, he hurried forward. He saw the van driver's face, saw him turning the wheel. The van caught him, too, spinning him round and flinging him to the ground. He fell heavily, heard someone screaming, felt the weight of the van on top of him.

The weight vanished; suddenly he felt very light, almost as if he were floating up into the clouds of blackness that seemed to surround him.

Thoughts of Diane came into his mind.

Something else came into it too. He had seen the number of the van. He had to tell someone. He mustn't die before he had told someone, before he had seen Diane again.

He opened his mouth, coughed twice and felt the warm saltiness of blood on his tongue. He gasped and blackness closed over him.

★ ★ ★

Superintendent Heaton sat in his office, tapping a pencil on the blotter in front of him, half blaming himself for what had happened to the young constable, half realising that he could never have foreseen it, that it was an unavoidable risk of being a policeman. This wasn't true, though. Wheeler had been in plain clothes, not recognisable as a policeman. He had been run down because he had seen something that the van driver thought might identify him.

The awful thing was that it could have happened to any member of the public.

Wheeler had been taken to hospital. After the accident it had been thought that he couldn't live, but swift, expert treatment had worked wonders. Now, all that remained was for him to come round from his coma and tell them what he could.

That could take days, the doctors said.

The other person, who had been killed by the van, had been identified as Dick Norden, Roxy's assistant. His relatives still had to be traced and told; an unpleasant job but one which he couldn't avoid.

The phone rang. The caller was Mossop, the Divisional man and Wheeler's immediate superior when he was working in uniform.

'Nothing about Wheeler yet,' Mossop said. 'Thought I'd let you know we hadn't forgotten you.'

'Thanks. How's his wife?'

'Still at the hospital. Only been married about three months, you know.' He paused. 'I wish we could get our hands on the swine — ' He broke off.

Heaton said: 'I know. There's no chance that any other of our chaps were around at the time, is there?'

'None at all. I've had a call out since it happened, but no one's come forward. Not even members of the public, and there were enough of them about.' There was a faint touch of bitterness in his voice.

'It's a wonder there weren't more hurt,' Heaton said.

After ringing off he sat for a moment. There was no one watching Rawson now, of course; neither was it much use arranging for someone, for in the time that had elapsed anything could have happened. There was only himself to blame for this. He had let himself be numbed by the events, so that he had lost his hold on the case.

Injury to one of his men always tended to have this effect on him.

There was nothing he could do but wait and see what Wheeler might tell them.

21

Kicked-Around-Bill

Mick Cartney said: 'Who the hell are you?'

'My name's Bill Cunningham. I'm Mr. Rawson's assistant.'

'What do you want?' Cartney stared at him. Little more than a boy really, he thought.

'Mr. Rawson sent me to make sure things are all right.'

Cartney put one hand on the already open door and said: 'You go back to Mr. Rawson and tell him that things are fine.'

'I've got to make sure they stay that way.'

Cartney scowled. 'And why does Rawson think that they shouldn't? Does he think I'm going to hurt Jean or something?'

'I don't know what he thinks. He told me to stay here and he's my boss; I do what he says.' He picked up the chair on which he had been sitting when Cartney had arrived, and moved it a little away from the door. 'I'll stay here. I won't bother you.'

Cartney moved towards him. 'Listen — '

'What's the matter, Mike, he isn't doing any harm,' came Jean's voice behind him. 'I shall worry if you send him away. I shall think that you've some reason for not wanting him here.'

Cartney turned. 'Don't say you don't trust me either!' he almost shouted. He followed her into the flat, crashing the door shut.

Bill relaxed again on the chair, looking at his watch. It was half past twelve. For some time he heard the sound of an argument from behind the closed door, but slowly the voices quietened until he could hear nothing.

He had been surprised when Rawson had told him what he wanted, but he agreed readily, not because Rawson was his boss and he was afraid to do otherwise, but because what he had asked him to do made him feel important. He had rung the off-licence opposite his home and asked them to tell his mother that he would be home very late as he was having tea at a friend's, then he had come to the flat.

Rawson had told him that Cartney would try to make him move, but that he was to stay there.

He wondered what Rawson was doing, why he couldn't go to the police.

It didn't matter really. The important thing was that they couldn't help and he, kicked-around-Bill, could.

He settled himself more comfortably and wondered how long it would be before Rawson came. Footsteps sounded on the stairs at the end of the corridor. Bill looked up; a woman was coming along, a shopping bag over one arm. She stopped at the flat before the Dixons', looking at Bill as she stabbed at the door with a key, trying to find the keyhole. Finally, she had to look away, banged the key home with the heel of her hand and went in.

The corridor was very quiet. The smell of new paint was all around and the central heating was making him feel pleasantly warm and drowsy. He felt his head nodding and jerked it back up, blinking as he tried to keep his eyes open. For something to do he strained to hear the voices again, but there was nothing. For a moment, thoughts of a back entrance by which they might have gone out passed through his mind, but he dismissed them. If there had been such a thing Rawson would have told him, and anyway the girl wouldn't have gone without telling him.

Unless Cartney had forced her.

He stood up, undecided whether or not to knock at the door. As he watched it, it opened and Cartney peered out.

'You still here? You'd better come in for something to eat.' Without waiting for an answer, he went back into the flat, leaving the door wide open. Bill followed him stiffly, stretching. He felt like yawning, but couldn't.

A small table had been brought into the living-room and set before the settee which was amply long enough to seat the three of them. Bill sat next to the poodle, staring at it curiously while the girl brought in plates with rolls on them and lettuce, cucumber and cress. Each one was a miniature salad; Bill, expecting a cooked meal, was a little surprised at this, but he assumed that she didn't feel up to cooking anything. He ate three of them, drank a quick cup of tea and then, oppressed by the silence, returned to his seat outside.

When the door had closed behind him, Cartney said: 'How much longer do I have to live in this atmosphere?'

'Until Sonia's found.' Jean stared at him steadily. 'Mike, it isn't only you who isn't trusted. The police don't trust Rawson, they think he knows a lot more than he's told them.'

'But yet you trust him,' sneered Cartney. 'What does that make you?'

Jean flushed. 'If you don't like it why don't you go away?'

'Go away! And what would your precious Rawson think if I did? He'd probably have every cop in the country after me.'

Jean said: 'If you've anything against

him why don't you ask him to his face?'

'Perhaps I will.' Cartney stood up slowly, crossed to the window. 'Perhaps I'll go round to see him. Shall I tell you what I'd like to do to your Mr. Rawson?' He leaned on the window sill, gazing into the street.

'What would you like to do?' asked Jean quietly.

Cartney didn't speak; he gazed hard into the street, then smiled. 'I've no need to go round. Rawson's here himself.'

Seconds later there was a ringing at the bell.

When he had let Rawson in, Cartney leaned against the wall. Jean was on the settee, while Bill still waited outside.

'Come to see what I'm doing, Rawson?' Cartney asked.

'Perhaps,' replied Rawson evenly.

'Well, here I am. Not doing any harm, am I?'

'Not as far as I can see.'

Cartney said: 'Has Sonia been on to you yet?'

'That's why I came.'

Quickly, he told them what had

happened. The address to which the man on the phone had told him to go was a restaurant and because of this he had been told to wait until three o'clock, when the dinner-time rush would be over and the place shut. As that gave him an hour and a half, he had wondered what to do to fill the time. Naturally, the man had stressed the importance of coming on his own; he had made it sound the most important part of the whole operation.

After some thought, he had decided to go round to Jean's to see how Bill was doing, and to see whether or not they had heard from the man.

When he had finished, Cartney, still lounging against the wall, said: 'That's settled then, isn't it, Rawson? If you don't think that I'm up to any harm, why don't you take me with you?'

Rawson said: 'I was told to go on my own. If I don't do that Sonia may be killed.'

'I don't think so.' Cartney levered himself off the wall, came slowly across the room and sat down next to Jean.

'They want you to do something and Sonia's the lever to make sure you do it. If they kill her they've lost their lever.'

They?

Rawson thought: how does he know there's more than one man?

He said: 'Only one man rang me up.'

'Of course he did. How many do you think can speak on the phone at once? It is obvious that there must be more than one man. There always is in a case like this.'

Rawson was undecided. If he agreed to the suggestion he ran the risk of having Sonia killed. If he didn't agree, then on his own he would have no chance of defeating a gang of men. What would they do to Sonia if he took someone else with him? What had they already done to make her scream like she had?

Cartney was challenging him with his stare.

Jean, hands linked round her knees, was gazing up at him, pleading with her eyes.

He said: 'I'm sorry. I've got to go on my own.'

The uncomfortable silence persisted until he left at two-thirty.

★ ★ ★

Just before Rawson left the flat, the phone rang in Heaton's office. He reached out and picked it up.

It was Mossop again. Heaton listened, then hung up and turned to Field, who had just returned from an unsuccessful search for stolen cameras at Roxy's.

'Wheeler's come round,' he said. 'He's given us the number of the van that knocked him down. Have it traced as soon as you can, will you?'

There was excitement in his voice.

Field made a couple of calls. Ten minutes later the man from the Licensing Authority told him: 'The van belongs to a man named Simon Collins.' He paused for an instant, and then gave him Collins' address in a dry precise voice. Field thanked him, rang off and told Heaton, who frowned.

'Collins?'

'Maybe it was stolen.'

'Perhaps.' There was disappointment in Heaton's voice. He had expected the van to belong to Harry Spencer, hadn't realised until now how much he had been relying on it. He looked again at the pad with Collins' name and a Limehouse address on it, then said:

'But why should they pinch a van?'

Field shrugged. 'Unless they meant to knock Norden down and didn't want to use their own car.'

'Could be. Check this Collins with Records, will you? In the meantime, I think I'd better send a man round there, just to keep an eye on the place.'

While Field went to Records, Heaton spoke briskly on the phone. Ten minutes later, everything was arranged and a man with a short-wave radio was stationed near the restaurant with photos of everyone involved in the case. He would contact the Information Room when anyone went in or out, and they would speak to Heaton. In the meantime, there was nothing to do but wait.

Another fifteen minutes went by before the first report came in.

'The man called Rawson is ringing the bell.'

Heaton gave a triumphant smile and called to Field: 'I told you he'd lead us to them if we asked him about Spencer.'

22

The Spencers

In an upstairs room at the restaurant, the noise of the bell was heard clearly.

Harry Spencer chuckled softly and said: 'This'll be Rawson now.'

'Are you going to see him?' His brother Cliff was lounging back on a wooden chair, tilted on two legs.

'We'll both go to see him. I wish that fool, Harding, had had more sense.'

He was silent, thinking of the folly of Harding, the third member of the gang. After the phone call to Rawson, Harry, who had had no sleep for nearly twenty hours, had arranged that he would sleep first, then his brother, then Harding, but when he had woken it had been to find that Harding had gone out. His excuse had been that as a cop had seen them together on the night of the killing it would look suspicious if they all three

217

vanished the day after. He intended to go out for a short while, he had told Cliff, to let himself be seen.

He had taken a van belonging to the restaurant's owner, Simon Collins.

Harry pushed Harding from his mind.

'Let's go and tell Rawson what'll happen to the girl if he doesn't get rid of these cameras for us.'

Cliff nodded, and they went downstairs noisily.

The restaurant was dimly lit. Rawson had been let in by Collins, who returned to his own part when he saw the brothers, of whom he was afraid, coming down the stairs.

Harry gestured towards a table. 'Sit down, Rawson.'

Rawson moved slowly, and sat down. Cliff Spencer dragged up two more chairs so that he and his brother faced him across the table.

'Well?' Rawson asked tautly.

Harry smiled, a gentle, sneering smile. 'Don't be in such a hurry.'

'I'm always in a hurry when I'm dealing with people like you. Where's Sonia?'

'She's around, pal. Don't panic.'

'Did you ring Wesloe's?'

Cliff nodded. 'We thought that with them and the Press you'd have a bit of pressure on you. We sent you the picture for the same reason. You had to be ready to play ball with us when we rang you.'

Rawson's eyes narrowed. He had been trying to forget the scream, which must have been the last part of the pressure campaign, but Cliff's words had brought it back vividly. He glanced round the room swiftly, saw the tables lurking in the gloom, the half-open door at the back, a light on beyond it and the edge of what could only be a cooking range. He looked across to the back, saw the door and the stairs down which these two men had come, and saw the man who had let him in going up them.

He said: 'Where is she?'

'Don't panic, pal.' Harry's eyes narrowed. 'And don't get any fancy ideas about freeing her, either. You won't find her if you look and, even if you did, we'd get the pair of you before you'd gone very far.'

He stood up and went across to another table, returning very quickly with a brown-paper parcel which he tossed at Rawson. He caught it. It was very light and soft; the paper crinkled loudly as he touched it.

Harry said: 'A present from Sonia.'

Rawson looked from one to the other, then felt the parcel again. It was sealed with sticky tape; pushing his finger nail under the corner of the tape, he peeled it off slowly. The two men watched him, obviously waiting for his reaction. He pulled off all the tape, screwed it into a ball and flicked it across the table. He wanted to ask them what had made Sonia scream, but he was afraid of the answer he might get.

He pulled the paper from around the parcel.

Inside it was another parcel, wrapped in newspaper. In the paper was the dress that Sonia had been wearing the last time he had seen her. He took it out, torn and dirty, then folded the papers round it and left it on the table.

'What have you done to her?'

'We haven't done anything to her — yet.'

'What about that scream?' In spite of his fear, the question came out.

Cliff said: 'The scream was nothing. We just held a knife near her face and pretended to stab her.' He leaned back reflectively. 'Amazing how these skirts are frightened of anything happening to their faces.'

Rawson asked: 'Was she at Roxy's when you were there?'

'What do you know about that?'

'A little. I've seen Norden.'

Harry spat on to the floor. 'I don't suppose it matters. You won't go to the police. Not unless you want Sonia sent to you in little bits, that is.'

'So you did kill him?'

'He deserved it.' Harry's voice rose. 'He killed my brother in an argument over what sort of cut he was going to get out of some cameras we'd nicked. When Blackie didn't come back we went round and found bloodstains. After we'd killed Roxy we found the skirt, where Roxy had put her, in a box. We were going to kill her.'

'Why didn't you?'

'Because we needed a photographer, and she could be used to pressure you into helping us.'

'Why do you need a photographer?'

Cliff said: 'It must have been a funny position for Roxy. She saw him kill Blackie, she was the only witness, and he loved her.'

Rawson thought: and she hated him. It wasn't an enviable position.

'And what about Bradford?'

'Who? You mean that joker we knocked down outside Roxy's? He knew too much about us.'

'And don't I?' Rawson asked softly.

'But you can't squeal. If you do, you know what happens. Sonia gets cut up into little bits.'

Rawson said: 'What do you want me to do?'

'Nothing very much.' Harry leaned forward across the table, his voice losing the bantering tone which had dominated it up to now. 'Listen, Rawson, you know about cameras, don't you?'

Rawson nodded.

'All I want you to do is sell some for me. When you've done it you give the money to me. The more you've got for them, the less we hurt Sonia. It's as simple as that.'

'What about Sonia in the meantime?'

'Sonia stays here. She's the guarantee.' Harry's voice hardened slowly. 'Make up your mind, Rawson. Are you going to help us, or not?'

Rawson sat very still, his mind running over what must have happened to Sonia after she had left him the other day. He knew that she had a few things to clear up with Roxy. She must have gone round on the spur of the moment, seen him kill Blackie Spencer, and put Roxy in the position where he had to kill her to save himself.

But Roxy had loved her; instead of killing her at once he had locked her up, to play with at his leisure.

And he had been killed himself.

The Spencers had carried her off as a lever. When they had taken her out of the trunk where Roxy had hidden her, one of her shoes must have fallen off and been forgotten in the tension and panic of the moment.

The point now was, how could he get her away from here?

While this was taking place, Simon Collins, the owner of the restaurant, was creeping quietly up the stairs. Ever since the three men had woken him in the middle of the night, more or less taking over his restaurant and the spare rooms over it, he had been waiting for a chance to find out what they were doing. At last it had come. Harding was out, he knew, and the others would be tied up with the newcomer for some time at least.

Earlier in the day, he had thought that he had heard a woman's voice in the room, but he hadn't been sure until Harry had tapped him on the shoulder at lunch time and told him curtly that he wanted to use the phone. There had been a woman with him then, a scared-looking girl. The terror in her eyes had been the first thing that had struck him; the second was that not even the bulky man's overcoat she wore could hide her figure.

He left the room as Harry took up the phone; because of that he didn't hear the scream, nor did he see what happened to the girl afterwards. The first time he knew that the phone conversation had finished had been when he had gone upstairs to remove the dinner plates and Harry had told him to let in a man who would be coming to see them about three o'clock. Half an hour later he had seen Harding go out, and decided then that if he was still out when the visitor came, and if they left the rooms empty, he would go up and have a look.

He had let Rawson in. He had seen that the rooms must be empty, and had crept quickly up the stairs. From long experience, he knew every loose board on them and, although he also knew that the men couldn't hear the faint noise he was making, he was so afraid of them that he crept very slowly.

He went into the first of the two rooms. He had been here before, when he had brought up the meals, and knew that anything that they wanted to hide must be in the other one. He went through the door. As there was no light from the stairs here, and the windows were covered over, it was dark: he pressed down the light switch.

He saw the girl who had been with Harry.

She was bound to a chair on the far side of the room, her head lolling as if she were unconscious. Collins stepped nearer. This time she wore no overcoat, just a short white slip that offered no concealment. Simon licked his lips; his eyes travelled from her tear-stained face to the thrust of her breasts, then to the slim waist and smoothly rounded thighs.

He stepped still nearer.

Who was the girl? What was she doing here, like this?

He reached out his hand. As he did so her head jerked up and her eyes opened. They opened wider, and he saw horror in them. He opened his mouth, and as he did so, the girl began to scream.

★　★　★

The scream was heard clearly by the three men downstairs. In the silence that followed it, another sound was heard. Someone was trying the front door.

23

Callers

Rawson was the first to move. He jerked the table forward, hard, and stood up. He was undecided whether to go up the stairs and see what was happening to Sonia, or whether to try to get to the door, and the split second of uncertainty cost him the advantage he had gained. Harry, still gasping from the blow with the table, kicked out. His toe landed on Rawson's leg muscle, numbing the leg. As he stumbled, he knocked Harry's chair over, and the two sprawled on the floor.

Rawson struggled. Cliff had joined his brother, and they were both struggling to get on top of him. As he heaved, Cliff caught his legs, twisting them. He cried out with the pain.

Harry was on top of him now. Rawson reached up with both his hands, clamping them round Harry's neck, squeezing, half fearful of killing him. He heard Harry grunting, then felt pressure on his fingers as Cliff tried to prize them away. As Rawson struggled, Cliff brought up his other hand, forcing Rawson's hands and arms back. Harry raised himself, trying to roll him over. He was still on top; suddenly he broke off his efforts and brought his fist smashing down on Rawson's nose.

Rawson felt the splitting pain, thought that he cried out, knew that tears were filling his eyes. Dazed and only semi-conscious, he felt someone take his hair and begin to batter his head against the floor.

★　★　★

When Simon had first heard the girl scream, his one thought had been that Cliff and Harry Spencer were certain to discover him now, and would be sure to kill him when they did. He swung towards the door to meet the attack, then a thought crossed his mind. Unless the girl told them he had been here they

229

wouldn't know. After all, she had been left without a gag, and could be expected to scream when she recovered. If he hid before anyone came up, and stayed hidden, no one would know he was here.

He saw a pile of crates and boxes against the far wall.

Running over to them, he pulled some of them back and stacked the others in front, so that, although the pile looked the same, there was now a space behind it. He squeezed himself behind the boxes.

No one came.

The girl was silent again.

After perhaps five minutes had passed, Simon realised that no one was going to come and crept out from behind the boxes. He ignored the girl, and went towards the door, half expecting some kind of trap.

There was none.

He went down the stairs. He heard the sound of a struggle as he neared the bottom, and began to realise why no one had come in answer to the scream. The girl must be the stranger's girlfriend, being used as some kind of lever. When she had screamed the stranger must have taken advantage of the confusion to start a fight.

He went towards the door, seeing Cliff banging Rawson's head on the floor.

All the men had their backs to him, it was unlikely that he would be seen. If he went out and returned later, no one would ever know that he had been upstairs. He pulled open the front door and stepped out.

A hand pushed him in the chest, sending him staggering backwards. He saw two men; the one at the back had a gun.

★　★　★

Rawson was almost unconscious. At the sound of Simon's exclamation and the noise of the sharp command which followed it, he managed to open his eyes.

He saw Cartney come in. Behind him was a man with a gun, who crossed quickly to Cliff and swiped at him with the butt.

'Leave him and get up!'

There was a pause, during which Rawson lay on the floor with his eyes closed, trying to calm his breathing and the thumping of his heart. He began to breathe deeply; gradually the need for more air died away.

'Is this Rawson?'

'That's right.'

'Why all the fighting?'

'The girl screamed. He started a fight and we were just finishing it.'

'I see. Why did the girl scream?'

Harry said: 'You're asking a lot of questions, Harding.'

'I've a right to ask them. I'm in this as much as you and if you make a mess of things I get it too. Why did the girl scream? And why was Simon running out of the door?'

Cliff said softly: 'Because he sneaked upstairs and made her scream. He must have thought it better to get out and return later.'

Rawson opened his eyes. He saw the men standing in a small group, all of them covered by the gun, Cliff's hands were clenched and he was staring at

Simon Collins, whose mouth was half open.

'Is it true?' barked the man with the gun.

Slowly, Simon nodded his head.

Harding turned to Cartney. 'And who the devil are you?'

'I'm a friend of Sonia's sister. I knew that Rawson was meeting you, so I followed him to see if I could help him. I thought that Sonia may have killed Roxy, once, but it seems that I must have been wrong.'

Rawson managed to make sense of this through the waves of pain that still surrounded him. He tried to sit up, but someone took hold of the room and tilted it, so that he fell back on the floor, his hand rasping against the rough boards.

Cartney said: 'Can't you do something for him?'

'It's his own fault. We want him to help us a little.' Harding looked at Harry.

'We still got the girl?'

'She's upstairs.'

'Bring Rawson round.'

Cliff went off to the kitchen, returning

with a bowl of water. Rawson felt the sudden chill and wetness as some of it sloshed over him. He sat up. This time there was no dizziness, just a dull ache all round his head and neck. He supported himself on one hand, brushing the wet hair out of his eyes with the other. When Cliff looked as if he were going to throw more water, he managed to say:

'No thanks, I can manage.'

His voice was much stronger than he had thought it would have been.

Harding said: 'Get the girl.'

As the two men went towards the door, Rawson tried to get up and stop them, but all he could do was get to his knees.

Harding said: 'There's no need to plead with us, Rawson.' A smile twitched his lips. 'You've messed things up so far. I'm having the girl brought down so that you can see what happens to her when you make a mess of things. After that, you can go and do the job properly.'

Rawson stayed on the floor, holding himself up by one arm, knowing that the longer he stayed there the more the pain would decrease. If he had enough time he would be fit enough to start the fight again.

This time there was a gun to contend with too.

Footsteps sounded on the stairs and he heard the sound of Harry's voice. Harding glanced towards the door; instantly Simon Collins lunged at him. The blow caught Harding off guard and his gun hit the floor with a dull thud. Cartney sprang towards it, Rawson moved more slowly, intending to help Simon overpower Harding.

The stairs door opened. Cliff stepped through and slumped unconscious as Cartney brought the gun down on the back of his head.

Rawson saw Sonia, saw Harry grab her arm and pull her back. The door slammed shut and Harry's voice came clearly.

'Get the police, Rawson, and I'll kill the girl.'

24

'I'll kill the girl'

There came the sound of footsteps, two sets, going quickly up the stairs, then silence fell. There was silence in the room downstairs, too. Cliff was still unconscious, Simon and Harding were covered by the gun in Cartney's hand. Simon was gazing round the room with short, sharp glances, as if searching for a way out; Harding looked at the floor.

Cartney asked: 'Is there any way into that room other than by the stairs?'

No one answered.

Rawson pulled himself to his feet with the help of a table, and felt the blood pounding in his ears.

'The windows looked to be bricked up,' he managed to say. 'I had a good look before I came in.'

'Can't we take the bricks out in some way?'

Simon Collins spoke before he had time to answer. 'No,' he said very quietly. 'There seems to be bricks only to fool people outside and make them think that the room isn't used any more.'

'What the hell are you talking about?' Cartney growled.

'There's a sheet of wood.' Simon was gabbling now, in his hurry to say what he had to say. 'It's marked to look like bricks on one side and fastened over the window. You can't tell the difference from the ground, it's too far away.'

'How firmly is it fastened?'

'Not too firmly, you could knock it away.' Simon's eyes gleamed, as if he sensed that Harry might be beaten, and wanted to work himself in well with the other side in case he was. He went on to say that there was a ladder at the back which could be used to climb up to the window. There was no glass in front of the board; once on the ladder it would be easy to break into the room.

'Where's the ladder?'

'At the back. I'll show you — '

'Stay there!' rapped Rawson as Simon

moved. 'I'll find it myself. If I want any help I'll call you, but until I do stay here.'

He moved towards the back door.

Cartney said: 'I think I'd better do this after that knock on the head that you've had.'

'No thanks, I can manage.'

Cartney's lips twisted slightly. 'Still don't trust me, do you?'

'It's not that, Mike, it's just that I'd rather do this myself.'

Without waiting for an answer, he went out to the back where he found the ladder propped against a wall. It was long and heavy, and he could barely manage to carry it alone, but eventually he managed to drag it to the yard at the back of the restaurant, which was shared by the buildings on each side. He glanced up at the window and then dodged back swiftly.

The brick markings moved again, then fell away.

He saw Harry look out. He must have realised that there was only wood covering the windows and must now be expecting someone to come up this way.

Rawson waited, out of sight of the

window. As long as Harry stayed there he could do nothing without being seen. Even when he did move, there was still a danger that he would return at any time.

He looked up again; Harry had gone.

Quickly, Rawson darted out into the yard, then dragged the ladder nearer the window, keeping as close to the wall as he could. When he had passed the window he stopped, glancing up again. He wished that he had told Cartney to arrange some kind of disturbance on the stairs, but that might have meant harm to Sonia. He went to what would be the top of the ladder and lifted it, turning it towards the wall, then working his way along, raising the ladder higher and higher. This was the tricky bit; getting the ladder in position might take a couple of minutes and Harry could see him at any time.

If he was seen there would be no second chance.

He felt the ladder hit the wall. It was about six inches away from where he wanted it. He pulled it clear and worked it along, his breath coming in short gasps with the effort, his arms aching. Eventually he had it where he wanted it, against the window next door, where Harry couldn't reach it to push it off, and where he might think that it was unconnected with the restaurant. Once he reached the window sill he could step across to the other one.

He reached the top and stepped carefully on to the sill. From here, it looked farther across to the other than it had done from the ground; he was a little uncertain now that he could step across.

He was on the window sill, pressed flat against the grimy glass. Cautiously he edged towards the next window. If Harry looked out he couldn't reach him, couldn't reach the ladder, but if he had a gun, or anything that he could throw —

He had no gun, Rawson was certain. If he had, he would have used it before, downstairs.

Rawson felt his hands damp, felt his brow cool when the breeze blew on it.

He was afraid.

He was afraid of not being able to cross to the other window, afraid that, even if he did, he wouldn't be able to get into the other room before Sonia had been injured, perhaps killed, and afraid that, even if he did get into the room, he would still be beaten in some way.

He stepped across to the other sill.

He could see Sonia sitting in a chair, very upright, could see the man by the door, his back to the window.

As he landed, Sonia saw him. She cried out involuntarily. Harry turned, baring his teeth when he saw Rawson. For a moment, it looked as if he was going to stay and resist, but as Rawson ran at him, he dragged open the door and raced down the stairs.

He clawed at the door at the bottom as Rawson went after him, taking the stairs three at a time.

Cartney raised his gun to stop the man, but he was brushed aside. Before he could do anything else, Rawson was in the line of fire. Harry reached the front door. Rawson slipped on the bottom stair, saw him open the door, saw that Cartney couldn't stop him and knew that he would never be able to catch him himself.

Harry half-turned to look at his pursuers, then ran out of the door.

He ran straight into the policemen who were stationed all round the front of the restaurant.

★ ★ ★

'So that's it,' Rawson said, later that evening. 'Spencer and his crowd hi-jacked that lorry, intending to get rid of the stuff through Roxy and his contacts. When Roxy had the argument with Blackie Spencer and killed him, then was killed in his turn, they had to find some other outlet.'

'And I happened to be there,' Sonia put in. There was a trace of bitterness in her voice. 'I went to see Roxy to cut myself off finally from him, and he'd just killed that man.' Her voice broke. 'He knocked me out. When I came round I was in that trunk. I don't know how long I was in there before the Spencers heard my knocking and let me out. As soon as they knew I had photographic contacts they took me away.'

She turned to Rawson, her distress evident as she recalled her experience. Rawson slid his arm round her. His fingers touched her breast, then she rested her head on his shoulder.

'Thank God it's over,' she said, reaching up to kiss him.

He glanced over to Cartney.

'Don't worry about me, Brian,' Cartney said. He grabbed Jean and she smiled.

There was still the problem of Janet and the photos, but he pushed that from his mind. Right now, there were other things to think about.

THE END

THAT INFERNAL TRIANGLE

Mark Ashton

An aeroplane goes down in the notorious Bermuda Triangle and on board is an Englishman recently heavily insured. The suspicious insurance company calls in Dan Felsen, former RAF pilot turned private investigator. Dan soon runs into trouble, which makes him suspect the infernal triangle is being used as a front for a much more sinister reason for the disappearance. His search for clues leads him to the Bahamas, the Caribbean and into a hurricane before he resolves the mystery.

THE GUILTY WITNESSES

John Newton Chance

Jonathan Blake had become involved in finding out just who had stolen a precious statuette. A gang of amateurs had so clever a plot that they had attracted the attention of a group of international spies, who habitually used amateurs as guide dogs to secret places of treasure and other things. Then, of course, the amateurs were disposed of. Jonathan Blake found himself being shot at because the guide dogs had lost their way . . .

THIS SIDE OF HELL

Robert Charles

Corporal David Canning buried his best friend below the burning African sand. Then he was alone, with a bullet-sprayed ambulance containing five seriously injured men and one hysterical nurse in his care. He faced heat, dust, thirst and hunger; and somewhere in the area roamed almost two hundred blood-crazed tribesmen led by a white mercenary with his own desperate reasons for catching up with the sole survivors of the massacre. But Canning vowed that he would win through to safety.

HEAVY IRON

Basil Copper

In this action-packed adventure, Mike Faraday, the laconic L.A. private investigator, stumbles by accident into one of his most bizarre and lethal cases when he is asked to collect a fifty thousand dollar debt by wealthy club owner, Manny Richter. Instead, Mike becomes involved in a murderous web of death, crime and corruption until the solution is revealed in the most unexpected manner.

ICE IN THE SUN

Douglas Enefer

It seemed like the simplest of assignments when the Princess Petra di Maurentis flew into London from her island in the sun — but anything private eye Dale Shand takes on invariably turns out to be vastly different from what it seems. Like the alluring Princess herself, whose only character flaw is a tendency to steal anything not actually nailed to the floor. Dale is in it deep, mixed-up with the most colourful bunch of fakes even he has ever run up against . . .

MURDER IS RUBY RED

E. and M. A. Radford

William Coppock, a well-known jeweller, was found dead in his car which was half submerged in the River Thames at Henley. An inquest decided that he had died from misadventure. Two months later, for no reason at all except his legendary 'suspicious mind', Doctor Manson, Scotland Yard's homicide chief, had the body exhumed — and found murder; and a ring of remarkable frauds. It took journeys to Paris, Amsterdam and Burma to find clues which eventually solved the crime.